William Houston joined the Royal Navy at the end of World War II. Trained at the Royal Naval College, Greenwich, he became a specialist weapons officer. On leaving the service he qualified as a chartered engineer and as a chartered secretary and administrator. For the next twenty years he developed his skills as a company 'doctor' to good effect, by turning round a large range of commercial and industrial companies associated with international bankers Kleinwort Benson and, earlier, with Slater Walker Securities.

He now lectures MBA students and businessmen on turn-around and crisis management, and his work on the imminent financial collapse has earned him the confidence of many senior members of the financial and business communities.

William Houston lives with his family near Knebworth, Hertfordshire.

MELTDOWN
THE GREAT '90s DEPRESSION AND HOW TO COME THROUGH IT A WINNER

WILLIAM HOUSTON

WARNER FUTURA

To Averil

A *Warner* Book

First published in Great Britain in 1993 by Smith Gryphon Ltd
This edition published in 1994 by Warner Books

A CIP catalogue record for this book
is available from the British Library

ISBN 0 7515 0819 5

Printed and bound in Great Britain by
Clays Ltd, St. Ives plc

Warner Books
A Division of
Little, Brown and Company (UK) Limited
Brettenham House
Lancaster Place
London WC2E 7EN

CONTENTS

ACKNOWLEDGEMENTS   vi

INTRODUCTION BY LORD REES-MOGG   vii

1   THE BAD NEWS AND THE GOOD NEWS   1

2   INTO THE TROUGH   7

3   HEAVY WEATHER   21

4   *DEJA VU*   37

5   ANATOMY OF A CRISIS   55

6   THE TAMING OF GOVERNMENT   81

7   GETTING BRITAIN TO WORK   95

8   KEEPING THE ROOF ON   119

9   A NEW MENU   135

10   LIFEBELTS FOR BUSINESS   153

11   AVOIDING THE CREDIT CRUNCH   173

12   AN EDGE FOR INVESTORS   189

13   AFTER THE STORM   199

POSTSCRIPT   203

FURTHER READING   207

INDEX   209

ACKNOWLEDGEMENTS

Many have helped with their time and information for this book. Where possible these have been mentioned in the text but in any case I would like to thank the following:

Robert Beith; Jane Bradford; Iben Browning; Monica Bryant; Mary Cartwright; Richard Coghlan; John Cooper; Andrew Cowen; Brenda Dainter; Richard Fox; Evelyn Browning-Garriss; Teddy Butler-Henderson; Ralph Howell; Simon Hunt; Martin Jakes; Michael Jordan; Stephen Lewis; Tony Longstaff; Rupert Lowe; Jane Malcomson; Patrick Mansel-Lewis; Charles Milner; Marilyn Moore; Rob Morley; William Rees-Mogg; Malcolm Reynell; Guenter Steinwitz; Gill Taylor; Lorraine Thompson; Michael Way; David Whately; Michael White; Stephen White.

In addition I am most grateful to Edward Russell-Walling and Helen Armitage for their help with the text and to Robert Smith for his guidance with structure and style; I would also like to thank my agent Doreen Montgomery. Finally, I would like to thank my wife Averil for her unfailing patience and her help in so many ways.

INTRODUCTION BY LORD REES-MOGG

There are two ways of approaching the world economy. There are the orthodox economists and forecasters, and there are the unorthodox. Undoubtedly, William Houston belongs to the second school. He explores theories that have not been generally accepted by academic economists. He is interested in subjects such as long-term economic cycles, which have interested such major economists as William Stanley Jevons but are currently regarded with suspicion.

What reason do we have for taking the unorthodox economists seriously? There is, first of all, a general reason that the orthodox economists have been unsuccessful in their forecasts. The accuracy of prediction is a good test of the validity of a scientific method. The predictions of the orthodox economists seem to work relatively well in periods of economic stability but fail to forecast periods of instability and also fail to make accurate forecasts, even of the short term, during such periods.

We also have the development of chaos theory, which suggests from the point of view of advance mathematics that the forecasting of complex systems with multiple variables, such as the world's weather or the world's economy, may be theoretically impossible. Chaos theory postulates that minor variables may initiate changes in major patterns, which may dominate the result. This goes against the commonsense view that you can judge the outcome in such large systems by concentrating attention on the major variables, which can most readily be detected.

The unorthodox economists have all been fascinated by variables that tend to be excluded from the view of the economists in the universities or the treasuries and central banks of the world. One of William Houston's interests is the effect of the climate on the world economy and the effect of volcanic activity on the climate. Here one has a link between unorthodox economics and the conservationists' school. It is very difficult for the layman to know what is sound in the science of the conservationists, and what will prove to be unsound. Yet when one reads studies like Al Gore's *Earth in the Balance*, one sees that the area of discussion is very close to parts of William Houston's.

Al Gore is now the Vice-President of the United States, and he had access to scientific studies of an authoritative kind. Even so, he may have made some misjudgements, and his critics say that he did. Yet the basic argument, which runs from fundamental causes of climatic change, through effects of climatic change on food production, to changes in the world economy caused by alterations in food supply, is one that overlaps with important areas in William Houston's book.

I also find myself sympathetic to the view that politicians always lag behind events and to the search for free-market solutions to economic problems wherever they are possible. Professor Buchanan's work on the market and democracy seems to offer the best explanation of how politicians actually behave. A politician is a businessman whose bottom line is votes. Just as a businessman may be very far sighted but will be judged by this year's profit and loss account, so a politician may be very far sighted but will be judged by current election results. A business prophet who operates at a loss loses his business, and a political prophet who loses elections loses office.

This makes it all the more important for independent thinkers, who are not running for office and not even trying to turn a profit, to raise ideas that do not have an immediate application in political terms. They need to do so because you can not expect the politicians or the businessmen to do it for themselves, and they might become ineffective if they did.

The practical men of the world have to operate inside an envelope of ideas, which is immediately viable. *Meltdown* provides just such a package, which includes matters that orthodox people are going to reject, and no doubt, like all unorthodox economists, William Houston will turn out to have been wrong in some of his projections. Nevertheless, his rather depressing view of the future is at least an excellent antidote to orthodox projections, which have proved so wrong in the recent past and look like proving wrong in the future.

ONE

THE BAD NEWS AND THE GOOD NEWS

MELTDOWN is about depressions and how to survive them, which means it is primarily about people. It is largely people, in the shape of politicians and bankers, who cause depressions, and it is people who have to live through them. *Meltdown* describes how wise politicians can steer their countries away from financial crisis, how managers who want to defy adversity can rebuild their businesses, and how individuals who have the will and the energy can thrive in difficult times.

Depressions have a way of destroying the worst of the old order. In the last Great Depression of the 1930s, that 'worst' was speculation and debt. In the 1990s it is again speculation and debt, but now many more nations and their peoples are in trouble than before. Those politicians in power when nations enter a depression are seldom those capable of leading the recovery. It generally requires others, untainted by failure, to prescribe and guide the cure. Ultimately, however, it is not politicians who lead nations out of depressions but people who, through their ingenuity and the capacity to take risks, work hard to create new industries. Politicians can only create the right atmosphere for success.

'Those who can not remember the past are condemned to repeat it,' George Santayana wrote. Ironically, one of mankind's greatest follies is its belief that it does learn from history and that the mistakes of the past can never be repeated. If we believe that having been through one Great Depression, we can never go through another, we are sorely misguided. The risk of a worldwide financial crisis is extremely high. It could start in the United States or Japan and rapidly produce a knock-on effect in other countries. The US dollar is still the world's reserve currency. A serious run on the dollar would lead to a rapid rise in US interest rates, forcing other nations to increase their own rates to stop a massive drain of funds to the United States. If US interest rates followed previous trends, they would rocket to well over 25 per cent and then collapse. This collapse would be accompanied by a rapid liquidation of assets as houses, commodities and financial securities were dumped in exchange for cash. This would then be the start of a deep depression and a very slow recovery.

The likelihood of such a chain of events is high because, in 1993, the western world is caught between the vice of excessive debt in many nations and a strong probability of climatic change. Cooler, drier weather will cause crop failures and push up food prices, followed by higher inflation and higher interest rates. The ensuing crisis will be much more serious than anything experienced in the 1930s and certainly too great for the world's central bankers to control.

Meltdown explains why we could face this unique combination of excessive debt and high food prices. No fewer than six business cycles, the mechanisms that have controlled economies for centuries, all reach a low point between 1990 and 1995 – an event that has not occurred for at least two hundred years. The effects will be felt for many months, but thé impact need not be disastrous if those in authority understand the lessons of history and take the correct precautionary measures.

The Great Depression of the 1930s ended with a belief that governments could and should direct the course of people's lives. Several countries like Germany, Italy, Spain and the Soviet Union experienced dictatorship. In others, like the United States, the power of central government was increased, and the state took on many of the responsibilities that had previously been the domain of individuals.

Now, in the 1990s, political leaders are dragging their electorates down one cul-de-sac after another. One of these roads that leads nowhere is the belief that the state has unlimited funds or that taxpayers have bottomless pockets. In the early 1930s, the income of central government in France and the United States collapsed by around 50 per cent, forcing deep cuts in government spending. If this happened now, politicians would quickly find taxpayers withholding their support until the government put its own house in order.

Meltdown suggests how the power of the state may be cut, and the budget balanced. In the last depression, the British government reduced public-service pay, increased taxation and cut back on expenses. Because the state is now so much more involved in people's lives, such an exercise would be far more complicated. But it could still be done. It should include further privatizing and simplifying the provision of services, making those who can afford it pay for health and education, cutting public-service pay and pensions and introducing a system of negative income tax to replace the maze of present entitlements. However, the experience of the 1930s shows that the state needs to address three essential matters.

One is the provision of a comprehensive work and training package for the millions who will be put out of work. Another is the establishment of a floor to prevent a complete price collapse of the housing market through a new government-guaranteed fund that would act as a buyer of last resort. The third is support for the legions of basically sound small businesses that will fail through bad debts or other mishaps. There should be tax incentives for investors to buy the equity or debt of such companies.

We should expect governments to lean towards the right as they curtail public expenditure although there may be flashes of radicalism, similar to Léon Blum's Front Populaire government of 1936 in France. Those in power should remember that during the good times those with money are prepared to give some to their fellow men; in depressions they seek to keep every penny they possess. As the recession deepens there will be increasing calls for greater tariff protection and competitive currency devaluations as politicians try to protect home industries and jobs. Greater isolationism will weaken international organizations like the United Nations and may even lead to the break-up of the European Community. This would echo the 1930s, when the world was plunged into a trade war by the passage of the protectionist Smoot–Hawley Tariff Act in the United States.

While it raised food prices in the West, cooler and drier weather could cause near famine in central Europe and the Commonwealth of Independent States. In consequence, western Europe could be flooded with refugees, who would impose even greater burdens on extended exchequers. It could be unwise for the west to disarm; harsh times encourage dictators.

Businesspeople should plan for a recession lasting at least until 1995, by which time all excess credit should have been wrung out of the system. After that there should be a slow recovery. Depressions mean a period of falling sales, cash shortages and tightened margins until credit starts expanding once again. The availability of credit is taken for granted in the modern business world, but it is based on trust. Once trust has evaporated, as it may, it can only be regained through a slow process of testing and verification. Collapsing credit will affect not only business but also the housing and property market. However, if loans can be negotiated, interest rates should be at rock bottom; in the 1930s, rates were around 2 per cent in Britain and 0.5 per cent in the United States.

The companies that survive will have learned to run their organizations with the minimum of fixed costs, buying in additional services when needed. The very competitive market conditions will force a high degree of innovation, and there should be a variety of new business opportunities. Many of these will help individuals become self-employed. Technology has largely increased the potential power and importance of the individual. Technically literate and intelligent people can now command computing and communication capacity on a scale that was impossible even ten years ago. From locations of their choosing, they can serve clients spread over continents.

Those who are able to take advantage of this situation will be the lucky ones. Things will not be so easy for the millions of people not needed by new, slimmer company structures. Government work programmes and other initiatives will help the transition, but many will find it very painful to have to start up on their own without the security of a monthly pay cheque and other perks. Even as the economy emerges from the depression, full-time jobs will be in short supply.

The following chapters explain why the Great Depression of the 1990s is likely to happen and describe the form it will take unless certain steps are taken. They also show how to plan for and make the best of the tough times ahead. It will be an exhilarating period for some, one of profound change for many, and one that will present grave difficulties for those who cannot adapt.

Best of luck.

TWO

INTO THE
TROUGH

Anyone who was earning a living or managing a business in the mid-1970s or early 1980s will remember the economic hardships of those times – the way in which prices just kept rising, the uncertainties of keeping a job, the effort involved in winning every order, and the sacrifices, big and little, that had to be made to keep afloat. Although these were times many would like to forget, their memory plays an essential part in dealing with the business cycles of boom/crisis/recession/recovery that have occurred regularly since (at least) the 1790s.

The lean years of the early 1980s were followed in their turn by the fat years of the mid-decade. The stock-market boomed, unemployment dropped, banks and shops fell over themselves to offer credit, and profits and salaries grew year after year. And now in the early 1990s, so soon after the good times, we are once again in recession – or worse. Cycles like this are a fundamental feature of economic life, and most people can chart at least one of them in their recent personal history. These relatively short boom-to-bust cycles, like the one described above, are easy to recognize. They tend to have a life from peak to peak (or trough to trough) of a decade, give or take a year or two on either side, and are sometimes known as Juglar cycles.

But there are other cycles at work, less easy to spot. This is because they occur over longer time periods and, in some cases, because they are not manmade like the Juglar, but the products of natural phenomena, like the winds and tides, stresses beneath the earth's crust and even activity on the surface of the sun. Though we may not notice them at work, these natural cycles affect our economic lives primarily by influencing crops, hence commodity prices and, ultimately, inflation.

Each has its highs and its lows, sometimes with many decades in between, and as each slides into its periodic trough it can be expected to have adverse effects on the world's economies. Since they often act out of phase – in other words, they do not all hit their peaks and troughs at the same time – the positive effects of one may override the negatives induced by another. What is startling about the years of the early 1990s is that, between 1990 and 1995, no fewer than six of these economic and climatic cycles all reach their low points – a phenomenon not seen for nearly two centuries.

All cycles have periods of plenty when the weather is good for crops, and it is relatively easy to manage a business or be a successful politician. The 1920s in America was such a time, as was the 1980s on each side of the Atlantic; both started with a sharp recession but, in each decade, particularly in the United States, there was a rapid growth of output, the banks lent freely, the stock-market rocketed. Most were convinced that the boom times would never end.

They always do, of course. Towards the end of the 1980s, just as in the 1920s, the banks realized that many of the building projects they had supported with such enthusiasm would not show a return; there was just too much office space around in the big cities like New York and London. To make it worse, the British Chancellor of the Exchequer had been so concerned to match the pound sterling with the German currency that inflation started to rise, and the Treasury were forced to apply the brakes with higher interest rates – in both decades. However, this only accelerated a process that was inevitable.

In the early years of the 1930s and 1990s consumers realized they were overborrowed. They were being squeezed between high real rates of interest and a declining value of their main asset, their house, with the added possibility of a reduction of income through the threat of redundancy. In short, they concluded that the game had changed, and it would be prudent to save, not spend. And, to the frustration of ministers who wanted everything to continue as before, that is exactly what they did. Quite simply, people did not believe the politicians who forecast an early recovery.

Economists call this condition debt deflation or a credit vortex, which means that the underlying value of an asset like a house reduces faster than the value of the associated loan. Once this starts there is little governments can do to arrest the drift except perhaps to prop up a few essential parts of the economy.

It is no coincidence that the pattern of these two decades, sixty years apart, is so similar. But the America of the 1990s is quite different from that of the 1930s in one very important respect. Then the government had very few borrowings and so was able to create funds to bail out overborrowed public and private corporations, home mortgagees and farmers. Unfortunately, similar support cannot be expected in the 1990s. The US government has issued too many guarantees already to banks, savings and loans institutions, and to private sector mortgage programmes.

In addition to its swamping effect on ordinary people, the downwave (another name for debt deflation) also affects those in government and in business. In just a few months they have had to change their entire strategy to deal with conditions quite unimaginable only a few years earlier. Unsurprisingly, many are out of their depth, which accounts for various unwise, even silly public statements made by ministers and others who felt they were still in control. The naïve optimism of Chancellor Norman Lamont's 'green shoots of recovery' 1992 Budget speech was such that stand-up comedians now use the phrase in their routines. In truth, once a downwave starts it is almost impossible to arrest – unless governments, businesses and individuals are prepared and have almost infinite resources.

It need not be that way. Because cycles follow a predictable pattern, their different phases can be predicted in advance and acted upon in time to avoid their worst effects – and to benefit from their opportunities. Those who foresaw the financial panics of 1975 and 1980 took protective measures by cutting costs, reducing indebtedness and generating cash, and so did well; they were able to ride the recession better than most and used their resources to buy valuable assets quite cheaply. Those who did not believe in the existence of cycles – or had misread the signals – at best had to write off a proportion of their balance sheets. At worst they became insolvent.

If we are to choose the most sensible course of action, we first need to understand the nature of the situation in which we find ourselves, and of the cyclical forces that have helped to get us there. Even if history never quite repeats itself, it is foolish to think that the future can be completely independent of the past. So the purpose here and in the next chapter is to begin to introduce the quite extraordinary number of these economic and climatic cycles that are converging in the first part of the 1990s. There are six basic rhythms that account for the conditions experienced up to the second half of 1992 and give an indication of what can be expected. The economic rhythms are the nine-to-eleven-year Juglar cycle, the eighteen-year Kuznets real-estate cycle and the rather longer Kondratieff cycle. The climatic cycles are the Browning food cycle, the 180-year sun-retrograde cycle and a centuries-long weather rhythm established by Raymond Wheeler – call it the Wheeler cycle.

· THE JUGLAR CYCLE ·
BOOM TO BUST IN FOUR EASY STEPS

While business cycles occur with a more or less predictable frequency, they are neither equal nor even. Interest rates do not move evenly and neither do stock-markets – largely because in the modern age there is too much political interference and too many international influences. None the less, they do follow an observable pattern. The first person to note the repetitive sequence of booms and busts was the French economist Clement Juglar who, in 1860, published the results of his research into interest rates and prices in Paris and London. It took an Austrian economist, Joseph Schumpeter, in his great work *Business Cycles*, published in 1939, to name the cycles after Juglar. Observation reveals that they invariably repeat themselves every nine to eleven years.

The Juglar cycle has four phases: prosperity, crisis, liquidation and recession. The main prosperity phase lasts the longest, occupying around two-thirds of the nine-to-eleven year rhythm. The other three phases fit relatively equally into the remaining one-third. **Prosperity** starts with low, and then only modestly rising, interest rates. Inflation has not stirred, unemployment is high and the cost of raw materials is containable. As the phase gets under way, unemployment drops, confidence rises and people begin to feel more comfortable about spending money. Demand outstrips supply and new capacity is brought on stream to satisfy it, feeding growth by creating work and demand for capital. Getting into debt becomes fashionable once again. Indeed, this turns into a debt euphoria when assets bought on loans yield a handsome profit. Like someone high on drugs, the level of borrowings rises to keep the momentum going.

As the boom continues, people and businesses develop an expectation that the value of assets, like houses, will continue to rise indefinitely. Businesses can be particularly prone to this narrow view of the future, and many corporate boards find it easier (and a lot more fun) to grow through acquisition on borrowed money than by grinding away to make profits on their core business.

Prosperity is inevitably followed by **crisis**. The extra debt that fuelled the prosperity flows through to inflation, which the authorities try to dowse by raising interest rates – an attempt to kill the monster they themselves created by encouraging cheap credit. Those with high borrowings find their profit margins are squeezed and need more working capital to support extra sales. They and others in need of cash continue to bid up the price of the limited supply of funds and interest rates rocket. So it was that UK base rates doubled from 7.5 per cent in 1988 to 15 per cent in 1991. As the economic climate sours, consumers are less willing – or able – to spend money, and supply starts to exceed demand. Sales fall, further harming the ability of borrowers to pay the higher interest on their debt. At the crisis peak, borrowers can no longer afford the extra cost of money and demand collapses. Cash is then 'king'.

Crisis gives way to the **liquidation** phase. Every debt has to be settled one way or another. Either the borrower pays it back or they default, in which case the lender loses the money. Since this usually benefits neither side, sometimes they come to an arrange-ment – in a liquidation climate the debtor is in an excellent position to bargain for better terms. The recent wave of corporate-debt reschedulings and refinancings by UK companies like Heron and

Brent Walker are typical of this phase of the cycle. During the depression of the 1930s a number of companies issued bonds that could be converted later into equities – a sound strategy if timed correctly.

By this stage in the cycle, all confidence in the credit system has been lost. Enter **recession**. Interest rates and commodity prices, which soared with inflation, now collapse. Prices are static or decline, unemployment rises and business activity falls flat. Those with the foresight to have become liquid – those, that is, who have converted their assets or investments into cash – before the crisis phase are now cash rich and can afford to buy assets very cheaply. Slowly, very slowly, confidence returns. Consumers, who have been saving instead of spending, start returning to the shops. There are not enough goods to satisfy the growing demand, business begins to invest in new manufacturing capacity, and a new phase of prosperity gets under way.

The first Juglar to follow the Great War started with the commodity panic of 1919 and ran until 1929, ending with a sharp reversal of interest rates after the stock-market crash of that year. The next two cycles ended in 1940 and 1950 respectively, although rises in interest rates normally associated with the crisis phase were masked by wartime controls. After World War II the next reversal was in 1955, when the Kuznets real-estate cycle (see below) ended. Since the mid-1950s, the cycles have become progressively more intense and the interest rate swings more violent, as shown by the successive peaks in 1960, 1970, 1974 (the result of a different cycle, the Kuznets, described below) and 1982, each of which has been higher than the last. On present showing, the end of the current cycle, whose recovery phase began in the UK in 1983, will be in 1993 or 1994.

· THE KUZNETS CYCLE ·
RHYTHM OF REAL ESTATE

During the 1930s Simon Kuznets, an American economist, traced the fortunes of US construction back into the mid-nineteenth century and discovered a recurring cycle of between eighteen and twenty years duration. Since World War II, this cycle has been apparent in Europe as well, and in Britain in particular, not least because of its relatively high levels of home ownership.

The housing cycle has a momentum of its own, connected with the amount of discretionary income available to be spent on homes, but not entirely dependent on the Juglar. The earliest low point of the Kuznets cycle that can be clearly identified was in 1865, marking the bottom of the housing rhythm in the United States. In this century it reached a low point around 1900, followed by another in 1918 – 19 during the raging post-war inflation. The biggest housing crash in the United States was from 1927 to 1934, when house building fell by 87 per cent – particularly after the Florida land speculation during the late 1920s. Because the Kuznets is not the only economic cycle at work, it is not always easy to distinguish among the regular rallies and declines of the Juglar. And in fact the Kuznets low of 1937 had little visible impact on the housing market on either side of the Atlantic.

Although the war and the ups and downs of the post-war period muddied the water somewhat, the low of the mid-1950s was more noticeable in both countries, cutting construction in Britain by 20 per cent and in the United States by somewhat less than 15 per cent. The last real-estate crash in the US coincided with the Kuznets low of 1974 and was echoed at the same time in Britain. In both countries the construction bubble burst, and major banks that had lent to property speculators were obliged to write off huge non-performing loans. The US housing market fell by 35 per cent, but the decline was less marked in Britain where construction finally collapsed with the Juglar low point in 1981.

The post-war boom in property finally ended with a vengeance in 1989-90. But the worst may not yet be over. The next low point of the Kuznets cycle will be in 1993. Between 1993 and 1995 both the Kuznets and the long-wave Kondratieff cycles (see below) reach their low point together, the first time this has happened since the 1840s. The evidence from both sides of the Atlantic of falling house prices, non-performing bank loans and the collapse of the US savings and loans institutions (building societies) already indicates a crash more severe than that of 1974. If the US pattern of the early 1930s is repeated, house prices on both sides of the Atlantic could fall over 70 per cent from 1989 levels without some form of government intervention.

The cycle is, on the face of it, linked to inflation, which erodes discretionary income and forces up interest rates. Both factors are hostile to the housing market, and housing declines as a result. The sad fact is that, in the short term, housing investment is not a hedge against rising prices – neither in Britain nor in the United States.

Although Kuznets himself did not connect the two, his cycle has now in fact been shown to be related to the lunar precession cycle of 18.6 years. This is the rhythm with which the moon shifts its angle to the equator as it orbits the earth. Dr Louis Thompson of Iowa State University shows in the July/August 1989 edition of the US magazine *Cycles* that the greatest effect upon the earth – on the tides, to be precise – occurs every 18.6 years. As will be explained in more detail in the section on Browning food cycles, tidal peaks magnify volcanic activity. Heightened volcanic activity produces weather changes, which result in lower food production. Less food means higher food prices, which means higher inflation.

· THE KONDRATIEFF CYCLE ·
TUNING IN TO THE LONG WAVE

Nicolai Kondratieff, an economist in the Moscow Agricultural Academy during the 1920s, was the first to recognize the long wave at work in the world economy. Kondratieff imprudently displeased his superior, one Joseph Stalin, by pointing out that although the imperialist economies would be hit during the 1930s, the history of commodity prices and interest rates from the eighteenth century onwards showed that they would recover. This provocative denial of the imminent death of capitalism, coupled with Kondratieff's sympathy for the lot of the Russian peasant farmer, led to his premature and solitary death in Siberia.

Kondratieff's work was first published in English during 1935, in the *Review of Economic Statistics* under the title 'The Long Wave in Economic Life'. Economist Joseph Schumpeter later dubbed this long wave the Kondratieff cycle, and showed how, ideally, six Juglar cycles fitted into one Kondratieff.

Kondratieff gave no reasons for his ideas. He only observed that events like periods of prosperity and depression, wars and good and bad harvests happen with regularity during the cycle. Other commentators have been more forthright. Schumpeter ventured the view that long waves were connected with the lag between invention and innovation. He gave as an example Abraham Darby's invention of the blast furnace early in the eighteenth century – and the fact that it only came into widespread use sixty years later. Irving Fisher, an American economist who advised people to invest in the stock-market on the eve of the Great Crash, thought it was a credit cycle, that is one of credit build up and collapse. He got that one right. It was – as we are discovering in the 1990s.

Others, such as US economist W. W. Rostow, identified the long wave as an investment cycle, in which consumer goods are produced in the upwave and infrastructure investment takes place in the downwave. Today a number of economists argue, correctly, that it takes a long wave to eliminate all the really large bad debts and unsafe companies that escaped the periodic Juglar cycles. While in the 1920s it was the Van Sweringen and Clarence Hatry empires that crashed, today it is the Polly Peck, Maxwell and Olympia & York edifices. Others have yet to totter and fall from their excesses of the past decade.

THE LONG WAVE IN HISTORY

As Jay W. Forrester, a business professor at the Massachusetts Institute of Technology, has pointed out in the April 1988 issue of *Cycles*, the main engine of the long wave is overinvestment or underinvestment in homes and factories, and all the associated investment in goods that goes with it. This occurs in much the same way as the short-wave Juglar cycle, but on a much broader scale and under the slower, more inexorable influence of other factors like climatic change. The effects of the long wave are apparent in the behaviour of the shorter business cycles, too. During the upwave of a Kondratieff cycle, the inherent shortage of productive capacity limits the Juglar's upsides while growing demand curbs the downsides. At the peak, however, and during the downwave the cycles become more extreme. Excessive capacity allows overexpansion during recoveries, and slowing demand deepens each successive recession. So the strong UK recovery after 1983, paradoxically enough, was typical of a long-wave downturn. And, as we noted earlier, interest rate peaks have become successively higher since the 1960s – the current long wave peaked in around 1965.

The years between the peak of a long wave and its next trough, as underlying economic conditions worsen, are characterized by heightened international and domestic conflict. Wars of expansion tend to occur at or after the peaks, often as a means of distracting the populace from a stagnant or worsening economy. Rebellions tend to happen further down the curve, as economic hardship and famine mean that the discontented have little to lose.

There is quite a consistent pattern of events between the peaks and troughs of each cycle. There have been four Kondratieff cycles since the late eighteenth century – the fourth is now coming to an end. If each cycle is given a 'K' number, K1 stretched from the low of the French Revolution to the next nadir in 1848 when Europe was beset by rebellions. During the upwave there was a major boom of cotton and pig-iron production in Britain carried by extensive canal networks. The railway boom took place in the downwave before the famines of the 'Hungry Forties'. Apart from the French Revolution, K1 saw at its peak in 1817 a spate of rebellions in Latin America, Greece, Belgium and other parts of Europe, following the Congress of Vienna. The wave ended with the Mexican and Crimean wars of the 1840s and early 1850s. The French and German revolts took place at the bottom of the wave in 1848.

As K2 moved into its upwave, we had the first Gold Rush of the 1850s, the American Civil War and the US rail boom, which lasted until the deep depression of the 1890s – which wiped out the stock speculators produced by the second Gold Rush in the 1880s. The Franco-Prussian war was at the peak of K2, and the Spanish American and Anglo-Boer wars were at its trough.

The next cycle, K3, kicked off with a boom that started in the Edwardian era. The Great War took place at its peak, as did the Russian Revolution. The subsequent 'Roaring Twenties' pre-ceded the Great Depression of the 1930s. World War II and the Spanish Civil War occurred at the low point.

The present wave, K4, started in 1939. US war production carried the upwave, with some short down periods, through to the end of the Vietnam War. The recession of the mid-1970s came after the cycle mid-point (around 1965), and the Reagan boom of the 1980s ended in 1990 in the same way that the 1920s gave way to the 1930s. The Korean and Vietnam Wars were around the peak of the cycle. Now, as we head for the trough, we see civil war and rebellions in the Balkans and, increasingly, in the former Soviet Union, the latter which, for ease of reference rather than total accuracy, we shall refer to throughout as the Commonwealth of Independent States (CIS).

Taking the maximum length of a long-wave cycle as sixty years, the next low point will be around 1995. The debts accumulated by people, businesses and governments during the upwave are more severe than in the 1930s, however, and will take years to unravel as we move into K5. There will assuredly be a recovery – though it is likely to be quite different from the one we expect.

THREE

HEAVY WEATHER

The way in which we have dealt with cycles so far suggests that they are determined by human behaviour. And so they are – to an extent. But if cycles are purely behaviourist phenomena, we ought to be able to find ways of smoothing out their effects. The fact that we have not managed to do this may be another example of human imperfection, but it is also because one fundamental influence on economic cycles is beyond our control – the climate. Many people find it odd that a change in the climate can alter business conditions. After all, how could a drop of a few degrees in Russia affect inflation? Why should a drought in Kansas influence UK interest rates? Yet the linkage between the physical climate and the economic variety is not only real but sometimes pivotal.

Like the expectation that debt will always be paid, there is an assumption that there will always be enough rain to provide crops. But, as many farmers in northern Europe were reminded in 1992, it takes 420 tons of water to produce one harvested ton of wheat. Too little water means a lower wheat yield, and less of anything essential almost always means that prices will rise – and that inflation will increase.

Unfortunately, politicians and economists are largely igno-rant about climatic matters. Most economists are only concerned with obvious economic and financial indicators, such as money supply, debt creation, inflation and the like. The more sophistic-ated will take wider political factors into account, but only a small minority even consider the phases of the climatic cycles that historically have had such a large bearing on the fortunes of nations. This is unfortunate, since some of the identifiable busi-ness cycles are specifically driven by climate.

Changes in the weather directly affect crop yields, often making the difference between a bumper harvest or a disaster. That, in turn, feeds into national and international economies through the price chain. When the climate is warm and humid, plentiful crops keep food prices down. So the cost of living is lower and more can be spent on consumer goods and services. When the weather becomes cool and dry, the growing season is shorter and crop yields are lower. Demand pressures on limited supplies cause food prices to rise, the cost of living goes up and less is available to be spent on so-called 'luxuries'. It is no accident that every Kondratieff low has coincided with a dry period in the northern hemisphere – sometimes warm, as in the 1930s, at other times cool, as it was in the 1840s.

If the weather has an effect on the economy, a whole range of phenomena – terrestrial and otherwise – have an effect on the weather. They include sunspot activity and movements in the solar system, tides and volcanic eruptions. This chapter examines some of these phenomena, the way in which they can influence food production and, indeed, the way they have done so in the past.

FOOD – NOT GROWING AS IT SHOULD

Until the 1970s, plentiful food was more or less taken for granted in the developed world. There had been huge increases in productivity, which more than doubled the grain output after World War II. Hybrid crops were developed to thrive in less than favourable climates, more sophisticated fertilizers added essential nutrients to the soil, and improvements were made to farming methods and irrigation.

If cheap and plentiful food were always available there would be no reason why the world's population could not go on increasing indefinitely. A larger population would provide more consumers and producers of manufactured goods; credit could be expanded continuously and the limitations that ended earlier prosperity phases would be avoided. In short, cycles would cease and prosperity would become an enduring economic condition.

It has not worked out that way. In many parts of the world nations have been unable to feed themselves – not least those where farms have been collectivized. Socialized agriculture may be partly to blame, but growing food shortages have also coincided with climatic changes outside man's control – notably in Eritrea, Mozambique and Zimbabwe, where starvation now stalks the land. Food production seldom keeps up with demand for long, and in 1991 the world's carry-over wheat stocks were the lowest for at least twenty years. What's more, the stocks are unevenly distributed and, when there are shortages, the growing country has less to export to others. This could be the position in 1993.

Foodstuffs primarily need adequate amounts of sunlight, water and nutrients for growth. The proportions vary from crop to crop, which is why hardy crops like wheat and rye grow in the upper latitudes while corn (maize) and rice grow nearer the equator. But even these general rules are not set in stone, because weather patterns change. The 1930s, for example, were particularly warm years when it was possible to grow tobacco in Canada. In recent times wine and corn have been harvested in Britain, something that was simply not possible in the nineteenth century.

Two major phenomena seem to be responsible for changing the weather patterns so markedly: volcanic action and sunspot activity. It is worth pointing out here that the Greenhouse Effect, supposedly responsible for a recent and steady rise in mean temperatures, has not been included in this analysis. This is largely because it has not been confirmed. In fact, a number of papers published in *Nature* magazine and elsewhere have demonstrated the correlation between the temperature anomalies experienced over time and planetary alignments and solar activity.

BLOWING THEIR TOPS, RUINING CROPS

In one important sense, the inflationary course for the early 1990s was set between 11 June and 15 June 1991. The event in question did not take place in Washington or Frankfurt. It was not determined in a bankers' boardroom or a parliamentary chamber. It took place in the Philippines and was hatched, if that's the word, in the bowels of a volcano. The eruption of Mount Pinatubo was one of the most powerful in history. It had a force of a 10-megaton bomb – or forty times the power that devastated Hiroshima – and the explosion hurled some 40 million tons of dust and sulphur dioxide heavenwards.

This, and other eruptions like it, caused immediate distress for anyone living near the volcano itself. But the damage caused extends many thousands of miles away from the lava flow. The point about volcanic eruptions is that they reduce the amount of sunlight falling on to the surface of the earth. These clouds of fine dust and acid droplets are discharged into the stratosphere, the atmospheric layer that starts at an altitude of about 50,000 feet above the troposphere. The sulphur dioxide contained in the eruption debris reacts with the ozone in the stratosphere to form sulphur trioxide. This in turn reacts with water vapour to form sulphuric acid clouds called aerosols. These are then carried around the earth by high-altitude winds over several weeks. The tiny particles stay aloft for many months – even years – providing an effective solar filter. The debris from Pinatubo spread mainly northwards, but even its drift to the south caused problems. Since it acted as a screen against the rays of the sun, it sent temperatures plummeting in many southern countries including New Zealand, where the extreme cold killed many lambs in August 1992.

While these eruptions can lower the temperature, they can also affect where and when it rains. They do this by altering the normal behaviour of the jet stream, the strong wind blowing in a narrow range of altitudes in the atmosphere that is responsible for much of the world's rainfall pattern. As a natural function of global wind cycles, cool air sweeps down from the poles, while warmer moist air comes up from the equator. The point at which they meet is known as the jet stream, or storm track, and, as cool collides with warm, it precipitates rain. Under normal circumstances, the jet stream – and hence the rainfall – is over northern latitudes in summer. Canadian wheat farmers are among those who have cause to be grateful for this. In the northern winter, the northern air temperature falls, and the storm track moves further south, taking its rainfall with it to irrigate the Texas cotton crop, for example. In the summer, the polar air temperature rises once again, allowing the equatorial winds to penetrate further north before their moisture is precipitated, and so the storm track retreats. A similar process, only in reverse, takes place in the southern hemisphere.

After a large volcanic eruption, however, the dust and aerosols drift towards the poles, cooling the polar air masses even further.

This abnormally cool air drifts south and now meets the tropical air much nearer the equator than usual – the storm track, in other words, has been moved much further south. Areas that would normally expect to have moisture now get cooler, drier weather and crops are poor as a result. Normally dry areas receive excessive rain. This means that, in the wake of Pinatubo, areas awaiting rain, such as the east coast of Africa, got very little while others, such as Argentina, were deluged. Pinatubo's legacy has already included storms in China and the Philippines, a drought in Sri Lanka and southern India, and a Colombian drought that was so bad that the country's hydroelectric power-generation systems failed. That in itself had serious repercussions for industry in Colombia.

Pinatubo-related problems for the northern latitudes may be only just beginning. As its clouds cool the circumpolar vortex around the North Pole they have already caused flooding in Texas and, in 1992, one of the coldest summers in northern states for years. In Europe, Spain has had torrents of unexpected rain while at the same time, in London, the winter of 1991–2 was the driest since 1836. The extremely wet and cold August experienced in Britain during 1992 was just another result of these changing weather patterns.

Volcanically induced or not, climatic change need not necessarily produce dire economic consequences. However, Pinatubo is likely to prove one of the five largest eruptions in the last 200 years. To gauge its possible impact, it may be helpful to look back at the effects of other volcanic eruptions – noting that, while they have occurred at different points along the cycle, volcanoes near each Kondratieff low from K1 to K4 have helped to drive recession into depression.

In the early morning of 5 April 1815, on the island of Sambawa in Indonesia, the volcano Tambora went off with the force of around one hundred megaton bombs. It discharged 35 cubic miles of volcanic dust and around 136 million tons of sulphuric acid into the stratosphere, all of which was rapidly carried north and south by winds. The effect of the dust and acid droplets was enough to reduce the amount of sunlight in the northern latitudes by 45 per cent. The year 1816 was known as the 'year without a summer', and there were widespread crop failures causing major depressions in North America and Europe. It may be instructive to note that, in the late summer of 1992, there were reports in areas of New England that the weather was the coolest since 1816. The weather in America is important to what happens in Europe. If the United States has a poor harvest, domestic food prices rise, domestic inflation follows and, given its size and economic influence, the country exports its problems elsewhere just as it did in the mid-1970s.

Tambora was the largest eruption for several thousand years, but there have been others, notably Krakatau in 1883. By looking at reports from weather stations since 1791, we can now calculate the temperature and humidities in the United States over the last 200 years. During that period, eleven major volcanoes erupted around the world, including the huge explosions of Tambora and Sumatra's Krakatau. Both are on or near the equator. In the southern hemisphere, only Tarawera in New Zealand (1886) and Azul in Chile (1932) were significant. The weather-station results showed that the climate in the United States could be affected for several years after a major eruption. The effects tended to follow a pattern. In year one the weather was colder than average; in year two it became drier as the storm track moved further south; year three was much colder than average and both effects could continue through to year four.

Europe has also suffered the direct effects of volcanic explosions. In 1783, and again in 1784, the Icelandic volcano Lakagigar erupted with a force equivalent to a one megaton hydrogen bomb.

On each occasion about one cubic kilometre of fine dust and vapour was projected several miles into the stratosphere. This drifted northwards and southwards over central Europe causing what is known as a 'dust veil'. In Iben Browning's *Climate and the Affairs of Man*, it is recorded that Benjamin Franklin, then US ambassador to France, described the sun as 'a bright copper-coloured disk set in a dull white leaden sky, not visible until twenty degrees above the horizon'. The weather became cold and very dry causing poor or abysmal wheat and grape harvests in France in the years 1784, 1786 and 1788. The French found it hard to accept a dearth of wine; a grain failure was quite intolerable and the citizenry came out in force during the bread riots of 1789 – riots which escalated into the French Revolution.

During the 1780s, the Japanese volcano Asama erupted twice in Honshu with similar force to Lakagigar. During the last decades of the eighteenth century, there were famines in India and China, and thousands of Mexicans died of famine after a late frost killed many crops. Two centuries later the most important indicators for the 1990s are the impact of Krakatau and Nicaragua's Cosiguina (1835). Like Pinatubo, both discharged an unusually large amount of gas and both occurred before the low point of the Kondratieff Cycle, deepening the slump in the US and elsewhere. Both periods were exceptionally dry, just like conditions in the early 1990s.

Cosiguina was not in itself very violent (in fact, it had only one-tenth of the force of Krakatau), but it coincided with a seasonally cold peak. For the next six years both the temperature and the rainfall in the US were below normal levels, causing crop failures and distress, which only aggravated the economic downturn of the time. Europe was also affected, with famines in Ireland and Russia (the Hungry Forties) and widespread unrest culminating in Europe's 1848 revolts.

Krakatau was one of the most dangerous eruptions on record,

causing much immediate and direct damage and drowning tens of thousands in a huge tidal wave that engulfed settlements along the nearby coasts. But its indirect, longer term effects were worse. The trade winds carried the dust north, reducing sunlight by 30 per cent in parts of North America and Europe. For the next four years, US temperatures were below average, and it was consistently dry. The net effect was to prolong the recessions of the 1870s well into the 1890s, the nadir of K3.

More recently, a Colombian volcano called Nevado del Ruiz erupted in 1987. It was a relatively small explosion, but its impact was considerable. It caused a rice failure in South-east Asia the following year and was largely responsible for the near dust-bowl conditions in the US grain belt in 1988. So we may await with some interest the eventual impact of Pinatubo.

· THE TIDAL TRIGGER ·
BROWNING FOOD CYCLES

If we accept that volcanoes have a profound effect on weather conditions, and hence on economic life, can we determine any regular pattern in their occurrence? Opinions vary about the triggering forces for volcanoes, but the late Dr Iben Browning of New Mexico showed that a high correlation exists between exceptional tidal forces, volcanic eruptions and earthquakes. He noted that volcanic action could be expected at those times when the alignment of the earth, sun and moon created earth tensions. Browning, who grew up on a dirt farm in Texas and whose grandfather was Cherokee, was an indefatigable scientist who worked on projects as diverse as cancer research and designing instrumentation for rockets. He also worked on the atomic bomb at the Sandia Corporation works in Albuquerque, which is where he first noticed the relationship between tides and seismic events.

There comes a point every 8.85 years when the orbits of the

earth around the sun and the moon around the earth coincide, exerting considerable force upon the earth. The attraction works on water – the one medium that can actually move easily – causing the sea level to rise to an exceptional level. The effect is not particularly noticeable away from land, but on the coasts nearest the sun and moon the additional weight and friction is enough to trigger earthquakes or volcanoes.

Some coastal areas are more vulnerable than others to this kind of friction. Around the Pacific, for instance, the sea bed is slowly sinking by a few centimetres a year, causing tremendous weaknesses in the rock structure. The San Andreas Fault is a notable example, but all the Pacific coastal areas are vulnerable which is why nearly two-thirds of all known volcanoes are located around the Pacific Rim – otherwise known as the 'Ring of Fire'.

Browning compared the exceptional tidal action on volcanoes to someone wishing to create a large explosion by bursting a boiler – volcanoes, after all, are large explosions. 'If the vessel is filled with water, the valves screwed tightly and a roaring fire started in the furnace,' he wrote in a neat analogy of the earth's inner structure, 'there will assuredly be an explosion. If someone arranges to hit the boiler periodically with a hammer – in the same way as the high tides pound the coastline – he will have arranged to be present at an explosion.'

Browning's research established the relationship between tides and volcanic activity, and he showed that tidal force peaks every 8.85 years, when both sun and moon are positioned to exert a maximum attraction on the earth's oceans. These forces add exceptional strains to coastlines already under stress from titanic forces below the earth's crust, which trigger earthquakes and volcanic eruptions. He also showed, however, that tidal–temperature relationship is modulated by the rise and fall of sunspots.

· SOLAR HEATING ·
SUNSPOTS AND THE WEATHER

Sunspots are areas of the sun – seen from the earth they look literally like spots – with a considerably higher surface temperature than the rest of the star, sometimes as much as 1000°C–2000°C higher. Added to the sun's mean temperature of around 6000°C, these variations have a significant effect on the warmth of the sun's rays reaching the earth. In parallel with these emissions, the sun discharges bursts of ultraviolet light, and long-wave radiation.

Nobody is quite certain what causes sunspots, although one theory is that they are the result of a cycle of magnetic intensity within the sun. They are certainly the result of some kind of cycle, because the temperature variations they cause have a regular high-low rhythm, which, having been measured with some precision, has been found to recur every 11.2 years. Particularly high sunspots have been experienced from 1989 to 1992, giving Britain an unusual (and welcome) string of balmy summers.

In much the same way as the cooling effects of volcanic debris are felt most keenly at the poles, where it is already cold, the warming effects of sunspots are felt most keenly at the equator where they heat up already warm air. And when high sunspots coincide with high volcanic activity, exceptionally cool polar winds meet unusually warm and humid tropical air. In this condition, the jet stream's position can change rapidly, causing violent storms, great hurricane activity and untimely frosts. It can also cause the dust-bowl conditions experienced in the United States in the early 1930s.

Browning collated the results of his observations of tides, volcanic activity and sunspots, defining an envelope of their high and low points now known as the Browning food cycle. Then he went one step further. He showed that his food cycle has a very close relationship with the Kondratieff cycle. Indeed, hc calculated that there was a 68,000–1 chance of the two cycles being unrelated. The climatic variations described by his theory almost certainly reinforce and explain the progress of the long wave towards its low point in 1995. Certainly, in terms of Browning's food cycles, the prognosis for grain harvests in 1993 is not good. It is highly likely that the coarse grains, such as corn in the USA and wheat in the CIS, will be particularly affected. Food shortages in what is now the CIS have explained much of the unrest experienced in that country throughout history.

The USA, CIS, Canada and China between them produce about 50 per cent of the world's wheat. An examination of their output since World War II, according to figures from the United Nations' Food and Agriculture Organization, shows years of significantly reduced output, which coincide with Browning's tidal force peaks. One was in 1974 – in the exceptionally dry year that followed, wheat production in the then USSR, for example, fell by 40 per cent. The next peak was in 1983–4, when US corn output fell by almost 50 per cent. The next peak is in 1992–3. While a poor CIS harvest in the coming year will further destabilize conditions in the region, poor US harvests will affect other grain consuming countries in the northern hemisphere – particularly those countries depending upon US exports.

Complicating the immediate grain-supply outlook is the fact that between 1979 to 1989 the area under cultivation declined markedly in the CIS (by 20 per cent) and China. Land removed from agriculture by the building of roads, towns or industry can often be used more productively than by farming it – provided that the food supply is adequate. However, much of the land lost could not produce crops again because of drought, water logging, pollution or climatic changes. Crop failure on a reduced area of cultivation could mean an even more serious food shortages.

· SPINNING BACKWARDS ·
THE 180-YEAR SUN RETROGRADE CYCLE

Curiously enough, though the sun is at the physical centre of our solar system, it is not at its exact centre of gravity but a little way to one side. This is because the mass of the planet Jupiter is large enough to force an imbalance. The result of this assymetry is that the real centre of the solar system (the so-called barycentre) makes an irregular ten-year orbit around the sun, without any apparent ill-effects. Except for once every 180 years, that is. On these occasions, instead of making its usual circuit, its orbit takes a short cut and passes on the wrong side of the sun. And on 20 April 1990 the centre of the solar system did just that. In technical jargon, it reversed its orbit, or retrograded, about the centre of the sun. This is a most unusual event, which last occurred in 1810 and before that in 1630. Each time it caused major earthly disturbances, and what happened then could well be in store for us in the next decade.

The 1630s were the middle of the 'Little Ice Age', a very cold period that primarily afflicted Europe. During the decade, there was the Civil War in Britain and the Thirty Years War in Germany when Gustavus Adolphus marched his army across the frozen Baltic Sea. At the same time, the Chinese Ming dynasty in China was deposed by hungry mobs. It was also a time of heavy volcanic action, as reported by H. H. Lamb in his book *Climate: Past, Present and Future*.

The second decade of the nineteenth century was equally eventful, coinciding with the middle of the K1 long wave. Europe was again at war, and there was a remarkable series of seismic disturbances, including the great 1811 earthquake on Missouri's New Madrid Fault and, in 1815, Tambora, one of the largest volcanic eruptions for several millennia. The weather was extremely cold, trapping Napoleon in Russia in 1812 and assisting Wellington in his final invasion of Spain during the Peninsula campaign. There were also famines in Switzerland and the Ukraine.

. . . AND NOW, THE THOUSAND-YEAR CYCLE!

One hundred and eighty years may seem to be pushing cycles to their limits, but in fact evidence exists for even longer rhythms. Raymond Wheeler was a professor of psychology at the Kansas State University when it was suggested to him that people behave differently in different climatic environments. Rather taken with the idea, he enlisted a team of 200 researchers including 95 historians to analyse 18 different areas of human activity from 699 BC to AD 1950. The work was started in the 1930s and ended, sadly, in the 1950s after Wheeler's death.

His results suggested that variables of temperature and rainfall are the most significant influences upon mankind, more important than geography or altitude. Categorizing successive climates as warm/wet, warm/dry, cool/wet or cool/dry, Wheeler and his researchers evaluated no less than 20,000 historical references. Historical events were correlated with climate by measuring the tree-ring widths of the ancient Sequoia firs growing near the west coast of America. The climate during each year of a tree's life is recorded – a good growing season will leave behind a wide growth, a poor year a much narrower band. Some trees have lived for many years before the birth of Christ and provide a unique and wonderful record.

Wheeler described how the four different climatic variations fit into 1000, 500, 150 and 100 year cycles. His papers explain how the 1990s will mark the end of the 500, 150 and 100 year cycles – a critical stage in the middle of the 1000 year rhythm. At the end of every five centuries – as now – there has been a reversion to a cool/

dry period, with a profound impact upon history. These are times of low rainfall and cooler weather, of poor crops, recessions, rebellions and civil wars. However, cool/dry periods have their compensations. They invigorate the human spirit, helping to remove the shackles of oppression. Wheeler forecast there would be a return to more fundamental values of faith and morals, and a flowering of democratic ideas that would release the individual from the powers of the state. Heady times to be sure.

Other periods have a different impact. Warm and wet conditions bring with them abundant crops, great prosperity, creativity, learning, great endeavours and wars of conquest. A typical warm/wet period was during the 1850s in America, which coincided with the first Gold Rush and the growth of railroads. This kind of exuberance gives way to conditions typically experienced during the 1930s. Warm and dry periods bring on the dismal condition of not only shortages and recessions but also the growth of dictators, left and right. These quell the human spirit, democratic systems collapse, freedoms are removed, and creativity is discouraged.

Finally, the cycle ends with another cool period. A cool and wet climate couples the vigour of cooler times with the growth associated with rainfall. Despotism is swept away and the individual once again becomes important. A typical period in Britain was in the 1830s when railways were being constructed and joint stock banks were started. It was also a time of social upheaval culminating in the Great Reform Act of 1832 and other reforms, such as the abolition of slavery.

If we examine past Kondratieff lows in the light of Wheeler's work, they tend to confirm the characteristics he described. Combine this with the influence of all the other cycles, and we can arrive at a prognosis for the 1990s.

During the 1780s and 1790s there was a spell of dry weather with crop failures bringing peak commodity prices. The massive eruptions in 1782 and 1784 of Lakagigar caused extreme weather changes and poor harvests, particularly in France. These contributed to the violence of the French Revolution. At the end of K1, in the 1840s the weather was cold and dry for several years and commodity prices peaked in England. The Irish Potato Famine was in 1842 – and in other parts of Europe the decade was remembered as the 'Hungry Forties'.

The 1890s, at the end of K2, were again dry and quite cold with high food prices in England, the United States and France. The 1930s were particularly dry and hot. Westerly winds blew across the Rockies evaporating ground moisture and creating dust-bowl conditions. The USSR suffered a major drought, with famine in the Ukraine and other grain areas.

The present rising earth tides are more reminiscent of the 1840s than of any other period during the last two centuries, and we should be anticipating a similarly cool/dry period, characterized by food shortages, depression and civil disturbances. As in the 1930s, people and politicians will become nationalistic and demand protection from foreign trade, civil wars can be expected, and governments will cut back on their spending. But at some time the depression will end and, if Wheeler is right, unlike the aftermath of the 1930s there will be a burst of freedom and a return to a democracy that has not been experienced for 500 years.

FOUR

DEJA VU

On 12 May 1930, the governors of Creditanstalt, Austria's largest and most respected bank, gathered at an emergency meeting to contemplate their situation. Overburdened with non-performing industrial loans and faced with rapidly escalating withdrawals, the bank was on the brink of failure. Reluctantly, but with little alternative, they called on the Austrian government for help. The government, with equally little alternative, obliged. The same day it guaranteed all Creditanstalt's domestic and foreign deposits and so forestalled a run on the bank. To many foreign observers at the time, the incident did not appear cause for worldwide concern. But, as the *League of Nations Survey* noted two years later: 'A crack had developed in the carefully constructed and patched façade of international finance and, through that crack, already timid investors and depositors caught glimpses of a weak and overburdened structure.'

Over the border to the north-west, German banks were in an equally fragile state. After the hyperinflation of 1924, the country was unable to raise long-term debt, and its banks could only borrow short-term money. Soon after Creditanstalt ran into difficulties, there was a run on the German Reichsbank during September 1930 when, in the course of four weeks, anxious depositors withdrew one billion Reichsmarks. Deposits continued to leave Germany until, on 5 June 1931, the German government announced that it could not continue reparation payments.

The storm centre now swivelled to Britain, where many banks had lent heavily to Central European institutions. Since the German financial crisis had frozen many short-term credits, worries arose over the health of these British lending banks. The result was that, during July and August, deposits began leaving British banks in gathering volumes.

In the two critical months to 21 September, the Bank of England made little attempt to raise interest rates to discourage this run on sterling. But the balanced Budget presented by Neville Chamberlain, Chancellor of the Exchequer in the coalition government formed by Ramsay MacDonald on 10 September, raised taxes and cut the pay of government employees. The ensuing mutiny of the Home Fleet at Invergordon, on Scotland's Cromarty Firth, on 15 September triggered even more cash withdrawals, and by 21 September parliament had approved legislation whereby sterling abandoned the gold standard. The pound dropped like a stone, losing 25 per cent against other important world currencies almost immediately.

Familiar? It should be. In 1991 several Norwegian banks failed, followed by a Danish bank in August 1992. Faced with likely bank losses over the next few years of over SKr90 billion (approximately £10 billion), the Swedish finance ministry was reported to be making contingency plans for purchasing the bad debts and setting up some form of depositor insurance. By mid-September, the currency markets were sufficiently concerned about the weaker European economies to start selling the lira, the pound and the peseta aggressively.

On 13 September Italy announced a 7 per cent devaluation within the Exchange Rate Mechanism (ERM – Europe's present-day equivalent of the gold standard), while the government desperately attempted to unwind its massive state debt. Shortly afterwards it withdrew the lira from the ERM for an indeterminate period. In the same week, Britain, unwilling to realign sterling within the system, also pulled its currency out of the ERM. If that was unnervingly reminiscent of its abandonment of the gold standard in 1930, so was the consequence. In succeeding weeks sterling plunged by up to 20 per cent against its previously fixed mid-rate against the Deutschmark.

Sterling and lira exchange rates fell because currency speculators decided that they were overvalued, and they felt safer in other currencies, notably – and ironically, since the German economy is unsteady – the Deutschmark. The immediate cause of the speculators' alarm was growing doubt over the likelihood of European economic and monetary union. That implied, more fundamentally, that the Italian and British economies and currencies would no longer be supported by its stronger neighbours. And the speculators had little faith in the indebted, low-growth economies of either country.

HAVEN'T WE BEEN HERE BEFORE?

The whole ERM episode was ominously reminiscent of the pound's departure from the gold standard sixty-one years earlier, almost to the day. Though it seems to mean little to our national leaders and their advisers, there are other similarities between the today's situation and that in the early 1930s.

● This is the most intractable recession since World War II. Normally the American economy could be boosted through lower interest rates and huge government spending. Yet with interest rates at historic lows, the economy is just scraping along the bottom.

● The ratio of total debt to the gross national product (GNP) in the USA peaked at 2.65 in 1931. It subsequently collapsed after the financial crisis that followed. By the middle of 1992, after rising steeply in the 1980s, the ratio was nearly 2.7, and we await the next crisis!

● In June 1930, President Hoover signed the Smoot–Hawley Tariff Act, which raised American import tariffs by 30 per cent and triggered retaliatory measures around the world. Now the farming lobbies in France and the USA are doing all they can to force an end to General Agreement on Tariffs and Trade (GATT) talks – which would result in a similar trade war.

● On 3 November 1992, President Bush was voted out of office to be replaced by the Democratic contender, Bill Clinton. Sixty years ago Herbert Hoover, also a one-term Republican president, lost to the Democratic Party's Franklin D. Roosevelt. Both defeated politicians held to the view there was no depression; their constituents did not believe them and voted them out of office.

● In 1931, it was the closure of banks that forced Germany to repudiate its debts and so cause the later financial crisis. A number of Scandinavian banks are in serious trouble today. And the possible collapse of Italy, whose government debt is over 100 per cent of the country's output, could cause similar defaults within the European Community.

● In the early 1990s, Britain has been passing through an exceptionally dry period, accompanied by fears for water supply and hosepipe bans in many parts of the country. The last comparable dry period in Britain was in the 1930s.

The financial fact of life so vividly demonstrated by the events of the early 1930s is that a credit collapse in one part of the world economy will threaten to trigger a domino effect. If the collapse takes place towards the low point of the 45- to 60-year Kondratieff cycle – which, in the 1930s it did – that threat will almost certainly become reality. But this time around it could be worse because, sixty years on, governments will also be faced with rising prices from the crop failures associated with the 1993 low point of the Kuznets cycle.

The combination of collapsing credit and rising inflation on many of the world's nations will be severe, to say the least. And much will depend on how their governments react to it. Judicious economic management will be painful but may succeed in avoiding the worst consequences of collapse. Vote-getting panaceas will ultimately both deepen and prolong the pain. The correct government action – extreme thrift – will not be easy because too many people and institutions now rely on state support of one kind or another for the austerities imposed by the British government in September 1931 to be accepted without considerable resistance.

The situation will be complicated by the fact that the difficulties facing governments will not all be economic. There are additional problems, the seeds of which are already visible. Western countries, for example, could face unprecedented refugee problems, driven by nationalism or famine. More seriously, they may be threatened by new and aggressive national groupings armed with nuclear weapons, who believe they can take with impunity from nations weakened by the recession. What we are looking at here is a process of major political, business and investment crisis, discontinuity and collapse.

This process has two important inputs, both of which are already feeding into the economic system – mushrooming debt and climatic change. We have already seen how the combination of these two powerful influences has affected the US economy before. Climatic change input has been dealt with in the previous chapter, so let us take a closer look at debt and what it can do.

· THE DEBT MUSHROOM · POISONOUS TO THE SYSTEM

If credit is the lifeblood of an economy, it can also cause arthritis. The granting of credit by one trader to another allows additional sales to be made that would not have been possible on a strict cash-settlement basis. This is all very well in times of expansion, but the position is reversed during a depression, when credit becomes arthritic. As traders know only too well, a large bad debt can cripple a small company and make life very uncomfortable for a larger one. So they are likely to restrict trade credit when there is doubt whether the debt will ever be settled. As danger of default grows, credit terms tighten, sales fall, more traders fail, and the downward spiral continues.

Loans are another form of the two-edged sword that is debt. In good times, banks and building societies lend extensively to expanding and acquisitive businesses, property companies and householders in the expectation that the good times will go on for ever. Borrowers, they assume, will be able to make regular interest payments and, eventually, clear the loan.

The 1980s were a shining example of the good times. But now, in the 1990s, the position is reversed, showing how quickly sentiment can change. Banks and building societies are now faced with the prospect of writing off huge bad debts from customers who can no longer afford to pay the interest – let alone the principal amount. Like companies and people, governments are not immune to the siren call of serious debt. The US government, for example, now has debts estimated at over £4000 billion – twice the ratio of debt to GNP that existed as recently as 1982 – and rising. During George Bush's four-year presidency alone, government debt rose by one-third. There is little evidence to suggest that Bill Clinton will be able to do any better.

In 1982, Ronald Reagan set up the Grace Commission, a group of businesspeople charged with investigating ways to cut government waste. Its findings, presented in early 1984, identified nearly 2500 ways in which the government could have cut spending by a total of $424 billion in the three years to 1987. The report has never been acted upon. The commission also warned that if these savings were not made, and if the federal deficits continued as forecast – which they have – interest on the federal debt would absorb 85 per cent of all the tax income from individuals and corporations by 1995. At a charge of $617 billion this would represent a payment of $1.7 billion every day of the year – or $7 a day for each US citizen of the USA. This would have to be raised either from the taxpayer or from even more borrowings.

Today, consumer debt in many countries is at levels not seen since the early 1930s. It is at its worst in Japan where debt per household is nearly 108 per cent of income. Britain is not far behind at 103 per cent while in the US the figure is 98 per cent. While high levels of private debt are hardly healthy for individuals, they are also dangerous for the economy in general because, in a recession, highly borrowed people are more likely to repay debt (thereby prolonging the economic malaise) than they are to borrow and spend (thereby assisting recovery). A combination of high private and public debt, as in the US, is the most frightening prospect of all.

Unfortunately, much of the debt has been incurred trying to revive the economy from the recession of the early 1980s. This has meant bailing out individuals and corporations with deposits in failed banks and savings and loan institutions (the so-called

Thrifts, the US equivalent of building societies). Through these rescue operations, the US government now owns $120-billion worth of repossessed housing. Through institutions like the Federal Deposit Insurance Corporation and the Federal Savings and Loan Insurance Corporation, the US government is committed to bailing out failed banks and savings and loans, although at a potentially terrible cost for its citizens who will ultimately have to foot the bill. Other governments, including Britain's, are in no position to run up the excessive public debt required to do anything similar. Even mighty Germany is having to resort to outside capital to salvage its new eastern *Länder*.

This is no longer a simple recession. Michael White, international political and economic consultant, describes the economic condition in the early 1990s as one of debt deflation – a situation in which the value of assets falls faster than the collateral debt. Debt deflation is a characteristic feature of a depression, and it changes the rules in a number of ways.

● During a business-cycle recession, companies run out of money and go bust. In a debt deflation, the number of bad debts is so large that the banks and other lenders fail alongside their customers.

● After a business-cycle recession, the recovery is demand-led. Confident consumers increase their spending, which moves through the inventory chain to manufacturers. They in turn start to increase capacity, invest in plant and take on help. In a debt deflation, disposable incomes remain flat or decline, and individuals are more inclined to save than spend. Recovery only starts once all or most of the debt has been wrung out of the system.

● During a business-cycle recession, people can expect to maintain their standard of living by selling assets that have held their value. This is not possible during debt deflation; asset values decline at a faster rate than debt, making it a buyer's market. This is the classic 'credit vortex'.

● Finally, conventional responses by central bankers to a business-cycle recession simply do not work in a debt deflation – indeed, they may well make matters worse. And it is extremely important that central bankers understand this. Reducing interest rates in a business-cycle recession often stimulates the economy by encouraging borrowing – but not in a debt deflation, as can already be seen in the US. In the same way, declining UK interest rates have so far failed to stimulate the economy. The real danger is a credit collapse from overwhelming bad debts.

OTHER TROUBLES IN THE WINGS

Highly indebted systems, as in the USA and the UK today, are especially vulnerable to external shocks, which further undermine efforts to recover. There are plenty of these just waiting to happen. Consider the following potential sources of shock.

Japan By November 1992, the Japanese economy was in the middle of 'a prolonged and severe downturn', in the words of the Japanese prime minister. Japanese banks in particular appear to be at risk. They are having problems with their loans – in the six months to September 1992, the bad loans of the country's top twenty-one banks rose 54 per cent to Y12,300 billion (£62 billion). They have also invested an increasing proportion of their depositors' money in the Japanese stock-market and so are extremely vulnerable to the effects of a market crash. This alone, which would almost certainly go hand in hand with a collapse in the overvalued property market (valued at its peak at around $24,000 billion), could destroy many banks. Enter the domino effect.

Given the extent of Japanese investment in US assets, the effects of a Japanese financial crisis would spread quickly as those assets were liquidated at knock-down prices.

Commonwealth of Independent States There is an alarming parallel between conditions before the French Revolution and the situation in the independent states of the Commonwealth of Independent States. Most republics are bankrupt, as France was in 1789, inflation is rampant, and new printing presses and paper mills are being set up to meet the demand for paper money. Food shortages are rife. At this stage of the cycle there is a high risk of crop failures, which could lead to serious civil disturbances and worse. Tensions between Ukraine and Russia – both well-armed – could create a civil war, which would have a devastating effect on world stability and create huge refugee problems, particularly in Germany.

Rise of nationalism Food shortages, expected in 1993–4 when important cereal crops fail, would accelerate the flood of refugees into central Europe from countries further east and cause major social problems nearer home. Rioting east German youths have already given a foretaste of the volatile reaction that can result when refugees are added to high unemployment, and attacks by German right-wing nationalists on foreigners are now taking place in western Germany. The effect of food shortages on the dispirited masses in what used to be the USSR could be extreme. Russia is already seeing the rise of fascist political parties, complete with SS-style uniforms. Although the authorities have moved against them, some of these are forming nationalistic, anti-semitic alliances with ousted communists – indeed, a number of the new fascist leaders are ousted communists.

Oil and gas supplies As the world's most important oil source, the Middle East is always a potential source of shock, and present political uncertainties make it more so. Rising Islamic fundamentalism, not least in the newly independent Moslem republics within the CIS, and the war in Bosnia merely add to the tensions and uncertainty. Although oil demand declines in a depression, disruption of oil supplies from the Middle East – or, indeed, of natural-gas supplies from the CIS to central Europe – could push energy prices to levels not seen since the oil crises of 1973 and 1979.

· STORM CLOUDS ·
WHAT TO LOOK OUT FOR

The crisis, when it hits, will not come without warning. There are a number of indicators that will tell us that big trouble has finally arrived. We can use them both to chart the progress of past cycles and to give us an idea of where we are in the present. Key among them is a measure of the yield on government bonds. A record of Juglar cycles through recent history is provided by fluctuations in bond yields, and among the most closely watched are the yields on long-term and short-term debt issued by the US federal government. Other indicators to keep an eye on are the Federal Reserve Credit and the CRB Index, a measure of commodity prices.

T-BOND YIELDS – A MAP FOR CYCLISTS

The money that all modern governments spend is raised from a combination of taxes and borrowing, the balance between the two depending upon the policies and skills of the party in power. Much like individuals and companies, governments with good economic records find it easier to borrow – and to borrow more cheaply – than those with bad. Where a country relies heavily upon borrowing, as the United States has throughout the 1980s and into the 1990s, much of the funding has to come from overseas. The conventional method is to sell government bonds to investors. The US finances part of its government spending by issuing Treasury bonds with a fixed coupon (specified rate of interest) and a redemption date (when it will be bought back) sometime in the future. Once issued, the price of the bonds varies with the expectation of inflation or recession. Simply put, inflation in the crisis phase reduces the value of money, and the bond yield rises. During a recession, the value of money rises as inflation falls, and the bond yield falls with it.

Yield is the return on a particular investment expressed as a percentage of the price paid for it. If the price goes down, the yield goes up and vice versa, but the original coupon remains the same. In this way, bonds change hands in the marketplace at less (or, in some circumstances, more) than their face value. Take a ten-year bond with a face value of £100 and a fixed coupon of 10 per cent – £10 in interest each year. If you believed that inflation would be lower than 10 per cent over the next decade, you might feel that to buy the bond would be a good way to protect the value of your money, particularly as your capital is guaranteed by the issuing government. You might even be tempted to pay £100 for it, which would give you a current yield of 10 per cent. If you expected inflation to be higher than 10 per cent, you would be inclined to pay less. If you paid £50, you would still get your £10 interest each year, but the bond would now offer a yield on your investment of 20 per cent – as a bond's price falls, its yield rises.

The yield of the US federal government's thirty-year Treasury bond (T-bond) is the most closely watched in the world, with good reason. The USA is still the world's largest economy and the US dollar remains the world's reserve currency – the ultimate safe haven, just as the gold-backed pound was in the nineteenth century. Unfortunately, the dollar is no longer backed by gold, but it is still used throughout the world as a means of exchange and a store of value. Any significant changes in the balance of economic power or in climatic changes will be reflected in America – particularly in the method of funding a government so much in debt.

The T-bond is a long-term security, in that its capital is only due to be repaid many years hence. So its yield reflects investors' long-term expectations of the US economy. The T-bond's short-term counterpart is the Treasury bill (T-bill), which is redeemed only ninety days after it is issued. As a short-term instrument its yield is much more closely allied to its coupon than is the case with T-bonds, and the Federal Reserve Board uses T-bills as a signalling mechanism to regulate interest rates, by setting the desired rate with each new issue. When T-bond yields started to rise in 1970, 1974 and 1980, this was followed shortly afterwards by an increase in the T-bill yield. The idea was to limit credit expansion by making money more expensive and so, ultimately, to quell inflation.

The T-bill tracked the bond yield well until 1990, since when, in an effort to revive the economy, it has been pushed down to near-1970s levels as interest rates have been deliberately forced down. There is invariably a difference between the T-bond and T-bill yields. Under normal circumstances, people expect the inflationary effects on their capital to worsen with time – so T-bond (long-term) yields are usually higher than T-bill (short-term) yields. This gap is known as the yield curve, and as long as T-bond yields are the higher of the two, it remains positive. After inflation has started to rise, the government will raise short-term interest rates, the T-bill yield will rise above that of the T-bond, and the yield curve will become negative; when inflation declines or the government wishes to stimulate the economy (by lowering short-term interest rates), it becomes positive once again.

Between 1919 and the present, the T-bond yield has shown

perceptible rises on more than ten occasions. Each time it has been followed by an increase in short-term interest rates. These rises tally with the low points of different business cycles in 1960, 1970, 1974 and 1981. There was an inflationary panic in 1970 with the low point of the Juglar cycle, another in 1974 with the low point of the Kuznets cycle, and a much larger one in 1981 coinciding once again with the Juglar. Each time the yield has increased more than the time before. We await with interest the next low point of the Kuznets in 1993.

Since World War II, the yield curve has been a good leader indicator of US recessions or recoveries, going negative in 1960, 1967, 1974 and 1979. Since 1991, we have had a situation very similar to that of the early 1930s when, despite a very positive yield curve, the debt deflation associated with a longer cycle prevented a recovery.

FEDERAL RESERVE CREDIT – RIDING FOR A FALL?

Federal Reserve Credit is the measure of the total assets of the Federal Reserve System, made up of government securities (over 80 per cent of the total), gold reserves and other assets. Between 1950 and 1980, bond yields and consumer prices (the US equivalent of the UK's retail price index – a measure of inflation) rose in line with Federal Reserve Credit. After 1980, however, as J. Pugsley points out in *Interest Rate Strategy*, there was a parting of the ways. Consumer prices headed sideways, followed by bond yields. But the credit curve kept rising, following the prices of financial securities. Pugsley describes this as the 'deadly anomaly'. At some point, the curves must converge again – either consumer prices (inflation) and interest rates will rocket, or the factors making up federal credit (the worth of government securities) will crash.

CRB INDEX – ADVANCE WARNING FOR INFLATION

Commodity prices in the United States are measured by the CRB (Commodity Research Bureau) Index, quoted daily in the *Wall Street Journal*. It is computed on a continuous basis, by taking the twenty-first root of twenty-one representative commodity futures prices multiplied together. The components include precious metals, industrial materials like copper, crops like wheat and imported materials like cocoa. It is a reliable leading indicator (advance warning, that is) for inflation and hence for the Treasury Bond. Indeed, the peaks of the CRB Index and the T-bond yield are closely related – the latter usually lagging by two or three months.

The Crisisometer below shows the relationships that might be expected. When the CRB hits the figure in the left-hand column, the T-bond should hit the figure on the right within two or three months. The T-bond yield can be found on the front page of the *Financial Times*, under the heading 'US closing rates: Yield'.

CRISISOMETER

CRB	T-BOND YIELD
200	7.24
210	7.76
220	8.20
240	9.30
260	10.20
280	10.90
300	12.90

The CRB is a particularly reliable lagging indicator of volcanic activity and its effects on climate and crops. Major movements in food prices – and hence the CRB – that have occurred since 1970 are as follows.

1971–4 There was a very large number of small volcanic eruptions between 1971 and 1974 ending with Tiatia in the Kuriles and Fuego in Guatemala. The soft commodity prices started a significant move in June 1972, about the same time as the T-bond and T-bill yield bottomed.

1977–80 The soft commodities started moving upwards after two small, but significant volcanic eruptions in 1977. Commodity prices generally hit a peak in October 1980, after the eruption of Bezymianny in Kamchatka and Mount St Helens in the US state of Washington.

1982–3 El Chichon erupted in Mexico during April 1982, and commodities started their rise in the third quarter, topping out up to a year later. The volcanic eruption, only a quarter to one-third of the power of Pinatubo, is probably the best exemplar for today. Then, silver and soya beans were notable movers.

1985–8 The relatively small volcanic eruption of Nevado del Ruiz in Colombia triggered a series of minor commodity price rises. Historically, the best leading indicators for inflation are the crop rises triggered by volcanic action.

In late 1992 the CRB Index was hovering about the 200 level. As the effects of the Pinatubo eruption continue to spread around the globe, we can expect the index to move upwards. When it hits the dangerously high level of 228 or thereabouts, we should be prepared for bond yields to follow. The crisis will be almost upon us.

FIVE

ANATOMY OF A CRISIS

The traditional government response to financial crisis has been either to clamp down on its own spending or inflate its way out of difficulties. In the 1930s the British government battened down the hatches on public spending and engineered a recovery for much of the country. By contrast, the German government's attempt to inflate its way out of trouble in the early 1920s was a disaster.

Today, the savings and livelihoods of many will depend upon the good sense of their political representatives, and advisers and their courage in implementing unpopular policies. In wartime, when fresh reserves are brought into the front line, they are immediately briefed by the veterans on how to survive the next twenty-four hours. During the American Civil War, for example, they would have been told it was generally safe to advance in the first thirty seconds after a musketry discharge, because that was how long it took to reload. In the Boer War they were warned not to light a third cigarette from the same match – that gave snipers time to spot them, aim and then pull the trigger.

Unfortunately, such survival briefings are seldom welcomed

by politicians and businesspeople entering a fresh stage of one of the business cycles. So their advisers, for the most part, tell them it will all blow over – which is what they want to hear. And, anyway, the only people who can well remember the last trough of the Kondratieff long wave, like the one we are now entering, are now pensioners. This is a pity because, right now, contemporary politicians and central bankers could do with some experienced advice.

As the world's financial situation deteriorates, a number of different things could happen. Depending on the response of government, there are three broad possibilities: unpopular spending cuts and raised taxes, a continuation of present policies and the inflation option – each of which could otherwise be described as grim, appalling or a total catastrophe. If politicians care to look, there are historical examples of each and its consequences. In the scenarios that follow, the US government is used for purposes of example, as the United States remains the world's most powerful economy; when America sneezes the rest of the world still catches a cold.

· SCENARIO ONE ·
PAINFUL CUTBACKS

The US government is led by wise individuals who have paid close regard to history. They have the intellect and courage to adjust the economy to continuing debt deflation and rising commodity prices by cutting back drastically on their own spending, particularly on the bureaucracy – unlikely action to come from its new President Bill Clinton. This would still imply a financial crisis, but for the over-indebted country it would mean a deliberate restructuring of debt and currency. It would also mean persuading the electorate that they had to adopt a much more simple way of life and accept a lower standard of living while the internal structures adjusted to a new tempo.

Since these wise politicians will have made sound contingency plans, they would follow any rise of the CRB Index or T-bond yield by raising short-term interest rates to quell inflation and stabilize the currency. The Swedish government used this strategy during the currency crisis of September 1992, when interest rates were raised at one stage to 1000 per cent. The US government would then move rapidly to cut its spending and to raise whatever taxes were necessary to balance the budget; any such measures would be very unpopular, but the administration would be ready for this. The final action would be to stabilize the currency by returning it to some form of gold backing after a major devaluation of the dollar.

It is possible that politicians could be jolted into corrective action by one or more triggers. These might include a final breakdown in the present round of GATT talks, a major national debt default (Italy, perhaps?) or a deteriorating food situation that pushed the CRB Index through 228, historically a critical level. To achieve this, the soft commodities like the grains are likely to rise first followed by the precious metals and others. T-bond and T-bill yields would follow commodity prices in terms of the Crisisometer in chapter 4, p.51.

The most successful example of this strategy in action was provided by the British government between 1931 to 1935. While it is true that many of the unemployed suffered considerable and unnecessary hardships, and the overseas stance was selfish, by 1939 Britain's GNP had increased by more than any other democracy except Sweden. While Britain's response reflected its status as a world trader, the US reaction – which was also, in the end, effective – was that of a self-contained economy. The French government, however, did terrible damage to the economy in the early thirties by applying a deliberate squeeze on spending to prevent the franc leaving the gold standard while other nations were devaluing their currency.

THE BRITS GET IT (MORE OR LESS) RIGHT . . .

A survival coalition government was formed in Britain in September 1931 by the Conservatives and a certain number in the Labour party. By and large, their policies served the country much better than the majority of other governments in their position. Between 1934 to 1939, the gross national product expanded by 50 per cent while many new industries were formed. Unfortunately the 1930s were remembered with bitterness by many in the old staple industries, such as coal, cotton, steel and ship building, which did not share in the recovery.

The US recession and its protectionist Smoot–Hawley Tariff Act was catastrophic for Britain's external finances. Between 1929 and 1931 exports of goods halved and overseas investment income declined by 40 per cent. The then Labour cabinet was unable to agree whether to deflate or inflate, and it resigned, to be replaced by the coalition government. The decision to deflate was imposed externally by the default of a German loan, which triggered a run on Britain's gold reserves. Parliament voted to withdraw the pound sterling from the gold standard, whereupon on 21 September 1931 it fell by 25 per cent against the dollar. Subsequent policy had two major strands – cheap money at home and trade negotiations abroad.

Before the devaluation of sterling against the US dollar the Chancellor, Neville Chamberlain, pruned back severely on public expenditure (including roads, education and local authority grants), reduced state salaries by 15 per cent and raised national-insurance contributions, so as to balance the budget. This allowed interest rates to be kept low, and the currency was stabilized by an exchange equalization account, which isolated interest rates from external currency flows. The policy was successful; lower interest rates meant that the government was able to borrow long-term funds at 3.5 per cent and short-term money at 2 per cent from 1932 to 1937. Industry could borrow at a small premium, and entrepreneurs thrived, building new industries, such as cars, commercial vehicles, domestic appliances, radio and aircraft.

The government applied its buying and financial muscle unscrupulously to impose preferential tariffs and bilateral arrangements on trading partners. Countries like Denmark and Argentina were obliged to buy from Britain in exchange for reciprocal trade in bacon, beef and wheat. A 10 per cent *ad valorem* duty was imposed on all imports, excluding most raw materials and foodstuffs. In practice, this meant a 20 per cent tariff on manufactured goods and even higher protection for iron and steel. On top of the devaluation of sterling, this created barriers nearly as high as those prevailing in the United States. The Commonwealth fared better than other trading partners. At its Ottawa Conference in 1932, a system of Imperial Preference was negotiated between the members giving each other advantageous financing and trading terms.

In contrast to the American response, little attempt was made to support industry, although cheap mortgage credit gave a boost to the construction industry. Some help was given to the staple industries of the North, Scotland and Wales through preferential export arrangements. The older industries were encouraged to replace obsolete equipment through grants, guaranteed loans and subsidies. The firms who took advantage of these may have become more efficient, but this did little to improve the lot of those made redundant. They had the option of staying where they were and living off means-tested benefits, or of moving to the developing South and Midlands.

. . . AND SO DO THE AMERICANS . . .

Probably the most successful recovery occurred not in the 1930s but in the 1920s, after Warren Harding became US President in 1921. He inherited an economy deeply in recession and did little but cut government expenditure by 40 per cent from the levels left by his absentee predecessor Woodrow Wilson. It worked. Low taxation and interest rates encouraged entrepreneurs to start new businesses, investment rose and consumer confidence recovered rapidly. The New York Stock Exchange started a rise, which hit an all-time high in September 1929.

This success was short-lived, however, and both Wall Street and the United States were soon to be plunged into the nightmare of the Great Depression, largely through the refusal of Harding's successor, President Hoover, to acknowledge the need for strongly defensive action.

President Franklin D. Roosevelt, who inherited Hoover's legacy, took the opposite approach to Britain, by trying to impose an almost fascist control over the US economy with his National Recovery Administration (NRA), which exalted the power of big business and the labour unions above that of the individual. Some parts of his New Deal (as his programme was known) were extremely successful, halting the collapse of credit and initiating some imaginative work programmes for unemployed people.

Roosevelt had to tackle three crucial issues. The 1931 German debt repudiation had triggered a banking crisis in Britain, which in turn started a run on US banks; in addition, the freezing of internal debt in the United States had slowed the normal commercial credit process. Then, between 1929 and 1932, farming income had dropped precipitously, threatening some 25 per cent of the population. Finally, there was a massive decline in consumer spending, which caused unemployment to soar and gross domestic product to collapse by nearly 50 per cent from 1929 to 1934.

One of the first acts of the Roosevelt administration was to declare a bank 'holiday', to stop the run on deposits. The banks, in short, did not open for business. The President informed radio listeners that the banks would be able to meet demand when they reopened, and this was enough to stop the run. Next came the passage of the Emergency Banking Act, making it illegal for US citizens to hold gold or foreign exchange – it was thought prudent to avoid a flight of capital, even though there were few other attractive currencies available. The Federal Deposit Insurance Corporation (FDIC) was set up to indemnify depositors against bank failures up to a certain level.

The administration then sought to raise internal price levels by devaluing the dollar against gold. Coming off the gold standard, in terms of which gold was valued at $20.67 per ounce, achieved an immediate devaluation of 7 per cent. Subsequent gold purchases by the Reconstruction Finance Corporation (RFC) raised the metal's price to $35 per ounce – effectively devaluing the dollar by nearly 70 per cent. The United States then returned to the gold standard for inter-governmental dealings.

Devaluation did little to raise internal prices, though it did succeed in increasing US exports and acted as a formidable new barrier to imports. Few foreigners held any dollars so trade was transacted in gold bullion – by 1939 the United States held some 60 per cent of the world's gold reserves.

While Roosevelt's financial measures may have given depositors greater confidence in the banking system, they did little to relieve the enormous debts that were paralysing the normal flow of credit. This was the job of the RFC, originally introduced by Hoover in January 1932 to support failing banks. Its scope was greatly enlarged under the New Deal to underwrite not only financial institutions but many public and private corporations. Funded partly by borrowing from the banks and partly from government deficit financing, its loans grew to total $5 billion, constituting nearly 50 per cent of the rise in public debt from 1930 to 1934.

Two important acts followed. First, the Home Owners Loan Corporation (HOLC) was set up to refinance parts of the private mortgage sector that was suffering 1000 repossessions a day by 1933. At its peak, the government was the mortgagor to some 20 per cent of the country's urban dwellings and did much to buttress democratic support from the middle classes. The HOLC was wound up in 1942, its purpose completed.

On similar lines, the Emergency Farm Mortgage Act (EFMA) was passed as part of a package of measures designed to help farmers keep their farms and shore up prices. The Agricultural Adjustment Act (AAA) sought in part to transfer additional funds from the consumer to the producers; food reserves were destroyed, and many animals prematurely slaughtered to increase prices. The AAA also provided cheap loans to farmers to buy machinery; many bought tractors, which only served to raise productivity and increase unemployment.

Probably the greatest failure of the New Deal was the National Recovery Administration, designed to inflate prices and wages by regulating production. It was conceived as a partnership between the government, industry and unions but was a disaster which seriously distorted the free market. Each industry was invited to draw up codes covering minimum wages, minimum prices, conditions of employment, output limitations and the like. The unintended effect was to create cartels among the major players in each industry and to push up prices faster than wages, while doing little to increase investment. In May 1935 the Supreme Court rendered it unconstitutional.

The most effective part of the NRA was the Public Works Administration (PWA), which created projects, such as bridge and dam building, harbour and waterway construction, sewage works and so on, that benefited the infrastructure. Large projects often do not employ masses of people, so Civil Works Administration (CWA) agencies were set up to clean up refuse, clear derelict sites and generally support the community.

The New Deal was the most comprehensive rescue plan ever to be imposed on a democracy in peacetime. It was hailed as a saviour by many and thoroughly detested by others. Aside from the disaster of the NRA, Roosevelt also brought in beneficial development projects. Some, like the Tennessee Valley Association (TVA), are still going, and others, like the Civilian Conservation Corps (CCC), were a great success and will serve as a model for today. The CCC is discussed at greater length in chapter 8.

· SCENARIO TWO ·
BUSINESS AS USUAL

In this scenario, the government sticks to policies that worked before the depression and allows debt deflation to run its course, letting the events of the 1930s repeat themselves for some countries. Debt deflation started in the USA in 1929 and continued until 1934, with the 1931 financial crisis in between. By the time Roosevelt became president, many banks had closed and depositors had lost their money.

In due course, New Deal legislation stabilized the credit collapse, but the economy made only a slow recovery before declining once again in 1937. The danger for the 1990s is that America can no longer afford debt-supporting programmes as proposed by President Clinton; nor can it stop a collapse of the dollar and a financial crisis if it attempts to reflate the economy – see scenario three.

A particularly dangerous form of sticking to present policies is an attempt to maintain existing exchange rates for an overvalued currency. This leads to unrealistically high interest rates and a progressive squeezing of company costs as they battle to remain competitive. Britain discovered this before leaving the gold standard in 1931 and was obliged to rediscover it in 1992. France discovered it in the early 1930s.

A signal that the crisis blow-off had arrived in the United States would be when the monthly average yield of the US Treasury bond rose above 9 per cent and kept going; the average for October 1992 was 7.5 per cent. Scenario two anticipates that the debt deflation will continue undiminished until all excess credit has been wrung out of the economy. This would require the T-bond yield to drop well below its April 1986 and December 1991 low point of 7.3 per cent.

There are many examples of politicians who believed there was nothing further to be done to bring their economies out of a depression. One was former US President George Bush, voted out of office in November 1992, sixty years after the president he most resembled – Herbert Hoover.

'AMERICAN BUSINESS IS STILL STRONG'

On the face of it, Hoover was one of the most qualified men ever to lead his country. From humble beginnings, he graduated from Stanford University as a mining engineer and made his fortune from prospecting around the world – not unlike oil wildcatter George Bush. Elected president in 1928, he responded to the Great Crash of 1929 and the start of the depression by announcing that American business was still strong – despite declining activity and growing unemployment. He created the Reconstruction Finance Corporation (RFC) to bail out banks, a focus which was ultimately shown to be much too narrow. Against his better judgement he signed into law the protectionist Smoot–Hawley Tariff Act, cited by some commentators as one of the single most important causes of the world depression.

FRENCH DEFLATION FALLS FLAT

During the 1920s France enjoyed a remarkable recovery from the hardships induced by war, and its output grew by some sixty per cent. Even as the United States and Britain began to struggle in the first years of the depression, France performed relatively well – it had wisely devalued the franc in 1928. This expansion was not to last, however, because when Britain and many other countries left the gold standard in 1931, France did not. Although it now had a balance of payments deficit, it still had massive gold reserves, and the government sought to restrict imports by applying quotas.

Faced with the dilemma of whether to devalue or deflate, it chose the latter. Between 1931 and 1934, prices and incomes were deliberately squeezed in an attempt to balance the budget and to align French costs with those of competitors who had devalued currencies. This policy did not work – after the US devaluation, foreign money started to leave the country, and France suffered the double pain of high interest rates and a continuing loss of gold reserves.

From 1932 onwards French gross domestic product was almost static, the budget deficit grew rapidly and unemployment, which had remained almost flat throughout the 1920s, started to rise. The last deflation attempt was in 1935, when the government, now headed by future Vichy premier Pierre Laval, imposed a further round of belt-tightening by imposing lower commodity prices. The discontent stirred up by the resulting wage reductions swept the Front Populaire government of Léon Blum into power. What happened after that could happen to any country after an unrelieved deflation.

THE LÉON BLUM EXPERIMENT

From the summer of 1936 until March 1937, France adopted measures similar to the New Deal, though without the financial strength of the United States or its social stability. The aim was to stimulate the economy, drive up spending power and increase government spending. It was hoped that the added tax revenues would balance the budget and allow more spending on armaments.

Following a wave of strikes in the late summer of 1936, French wages were increased by around 12 per cent, paid holidays were introduced and a forty-hour week agreed upon. This raised labour costs, which were passed straight through to prices, and the result was virtually no increase in the purchasing power of the workers. Export prices rose by 6 per cent, production declined by 9 per cent, and unemployment increased.

These policies triggered a flight of foreign capital and a sudden decline in gold reserves. Three months later France abandoned the gold standard and the franc fell by 25 per cent. The Blum government reversed the cuts in public expenditure introduced by Laval and initiated a FFr20 billion public works programme. The effects of this extra expenditure were almost completely nullified by rising prices and the flight of capital.

· SCENARIO THREE ·
THE MEDDLING POLITICIANS

It would be comforting, though perhaps naïve, to believe that governments would never again be tempted to inflate their way out of a depression. And yet deeply indebted governments like the United States, Britain and Italy might just believe that inflation was a good – perhaps the only – way of reducing their debts to zero, by making them worthless.

In the final scenario, the government believes that the squeeze between high commodity prices and debt deflation will not be tolerated by the electorate, so the politicians opt to spend their way out of the depression – otherwise known as monetizing debt. This has two effects, as the Germans found in the early 1920s: first, the currency collapses, but, second, government debt becomes worthless; as treasuries find, it is easier to make debt worthless than to repay it. Naturally, as money rapidly loses its value, this is hugely inflationary. Spending and the stock-market rocket for a time, but the collapsing currency eventually triggers a massive rise in interest rates, and the final deflation is much worse than it would have been had the politicians not meddled.

The mechanics involved in choosing the inflation route are simple. One way is for the central bank effectively to buy back government bonds in exchange for newly printed notes, which find their way into circulation by being used to pay for government services. Another is for the central bank, in exchange for new securities, to give the government a cheque, which is duly deposited in the banking system. The banks are then awash with credit, which they can relend.

Three phases can be expected – inflation, liquidation and depression. The **inflation**, which could start in 1993 and peak up to eighteen months later, is likely to be driven by increasing food prices or what the economists call 'accommodation', which is a polite word for the central bank's printing of money. In either case, the yield on the T-bond will start to rise. If it goes much above 9.5 per cent, inflation is well and truly under way. Another indicator could be the CRB Index rising through the critical level of 228. Finally, a sign that the Federal Reserve was accommodating even further would be a steep rise in the Federal Credit Reserve.

Once inflation has started, it can only be quelled by increasing short-term interest rates – a measure central banks would be most reluctant to impose during a depression. As the markets realize the government's reluctance to intervene, investors will pile into resource and inflation stocks and physical commodities such as gold. Inevitably, however, short-term interest rates will start to rise, stimulated by the need to stop the currency collapsing completely. The effects could be dramatic, with the T-bond yield rising to around 20 per cent, short-term T-bills to well over 25 per cent and the CRB Index – propelled by a rise in the precious metals, particularly gold, that could peak at well over $1000 an ounce – to over 400.

Inflation continues until the cost of money and the price of speculation become unbearable, and demand cracks. Prices that had been rising almost vertically come to a point in a dramatic 'spike', then fall as the **liquidation** begins. If history is a reliable indicator, precious metals and commodities will be the first to turn downwards followed by the short-term T-bills and, finally, the T-bond. Perhaps the most dramatic reversal could be the Federal Reserve Credit curve, which, after an almost vertical rise, would fall sharply when the Federal Reserve System can no longer issue any more credit.

Liquidation can be devastating. Assets like property, commodities, precious metals, objets d'art – everything that can be turned into cash – are liquidated to pay off debt. The steepness of the fall is almost invariably sharper than the rise because, by then, all demand has evaporated, and conversion into cash is all that matters.

After the inflationary peak and the liquidation phase comes the **depression**. Although it may not seem so at the time, a deep depression marks the start of a new credit cycle, which is likely to last a further forty-five to sixty years. As in the 1930s, there will be several false starts when recovery seems under way, only to peter out once again. The key issue is confidence – whether lenders will grant new credit or loans in the expectation that they will ever be repaid.

There are two classic examples of the inflation scenario in economic history – one in post-revolutionary France and the other in the German Weimar Republic. Apart from the damage they did the social fabric of their countries, both ultimately led to dictatorship. Because of the real possibility that the politicians may choose this road, and because of the utter misery it will lead to, it is worth describing both of them in some detail.

THE END OF THE *ASSIGNAT*

During the 1780s, France was run essentially by a council of aristocrats with the king at its head. It was in many ways a time of considerable prosperity: roads were the best in Europe, the administration was being reformed, industry was thriving, many peasants had been given their freedom, and torture was no longer being used to extract confessions.

Unfortunately, the country was also bankrupt. It had overspent on helping the American colonists win their War of Independence, and the administration was attempting to recoup its losses. The nobles and the church, however, refused to accept a rise in taxes. Instead this was to fall primarily on the middle class and traders through the payment of *péages*, internal duties levied on the passage of goods along roads, rivers and canals.

It was also to fall on the peasantry with their seigneurial obligations to the manor or castles. What was worse, food prices were rising as a result of crop failures and, by 1789, the worst-off were paying 80 per cent of their income for bread – up from two-thirds at the start of the decade. Matters came to a head over the 14 July storming of the Bastille, which acted as a trigger for uprisings all over the country. A National Assembly was formed as the court council disintegrated.

The underlying cause of the inflation that followed was the destruction of the currency. When the new government sought to buy the huge landholdings owned by the church in an effort to reduce its power, it issued *assignats*, a form of bond that later became currency in 1790. Steady issues of paper to pay for wars and other government expenditure reduced the purchasing value of *assignats* to 63 per cent of their original value by January 1792 and 22 per cent in August 1793. After a brief rally in December 1793, the *assignat* collapsed and became virtually worthless in early 1796.

As in other times of food shortages and collapsing currencies, farmers were not prepared to exchange their produce for worthless paper. The result was a proliferation of currency speculators and food hoarders. Again, conditions were typical of other great inflations. The speculators were able to borrow money on easy terms. This was then used to buy grain or some other easily traded commodity, which could be sold at an inflated price in a matter of months, the loan repaid and a useful profit cleared. Speculation became so widespread and food was so short that hoarding was made a capital offence.

After a period of grave disorder, inflation inevitably leads to either a collapse or a military dictatorship. In the case of post-revolutionary France, it was the latter, in the shape of young artillery captain Napoleon Bonaparte, who first came to the attention of the military authorities when he cleared the British out of Toulon in September 1793. A believer in the works of Rousseau and a keen supporter of the revolution, Bonaparte fought with distinction in the wars during the early 1790s. Coming to the attention of the new ruling Directorate, he was given command of the invasion army to Italy and after a spectacular success led the expedition to Egypt. Napoleon finally achieved political power after a *coup d'état*, which began on 9 November 1799.

A BARROWLOAD OF NOTES BUYS ONE CABBAGE

No one today can doubt the German Bundesbank's total commitment to keeping down inflation, but it was not always like that. Between 1920 and 1924 German politicians and the Bundesbank's predecessor, the Reichsbank, between them introduced a series of measures that in due course destroyed the currency, seriously upset the social fabric of Germany and ultimately ushered in World War II.

The starting point was probably the decision to finance the Great War of 1914–18, not through taxation but by the issue of debt and notes. The war cost Germany 164 billion marks, of which only 8 billion marks (or 5 per cent) was raised from taxes. It had been hoped that the Schlieffen Plan for encircling Paris in 1914 would see a swift end to the offensive without imposing a financial load on the public. This turned out to have been an unwise decision. The policy, dating from as recently as 1913, of backing the mark one-third with gold and two-thirds by government notes was abandoned. Instead, huge quantities of notes and bonds were issued; the notes in special war-loan funds, the bonds in the main to be bought by patriotic Germans.

After Germany lost the war, economic conditions were to prove disastrous for the country both politically and financially. The Allied wartime blockade had already reduced living standards by half. Many soldiers returning from the front found their families destitute – food alone cost three-quarters of a household budget, compared with one-half in 1914. The mark, which had been equivalent to one shilling, one franc or one lire in 1913, sank to half its value by 1918 and a quarter by 1919.

The disciplined nation might have been able to weather the post-war turmoil had it not been for the conditions of the Versailles Treaty. The worst of these were the reparations demanded – particularly by France. In October 1920, Lord D'Abernon, the newly appointed British Ambassador to Germany, reported that annual reparations would double the tax burden on the German people and that hard currency reparations would absorb 26 per cent of export income. The trouble was that German tax receipts were considerably short of expectations, because of tax evasion by some of the richer citizens and a huge deficit run up by the nationalized railways. The demands of the French increased, and, when no further funds were forthcoming, they occupied the Rhine ports and threatened further reprisals. In despair, the German government speeded up the process of printing money.

In June 1921, a new union-backed government led by Dr Josef Wirth was formed and the payments under a schedule agreed at a 'London Ultimatum' conference were duly paid. However, subsequent payments became a real problem, which the central bank believed could only be solved by buying vast tranches of foreign exchange – effectively fuelling the mark's devaluation. The move was supported by industrialists who were under intense pressure from a workforce wanting to maintain its living standards at a time of increasing inflation. As the mark plummeted on the foreign exchanges, the notes in circulation had risen from 35 milliard in 1919 to 200 milliard in July 1922. The authorities and sophisticated opinion in Berlin could see nothing wrong; they believed that the need to print money was the result of the mark's collapse – not its cause.

AUSTRIA PRINTS ITS WAY INTO TROUBLE.

In Vienna, late capital of empire, politicians tried to keep up the old lifestyle in much the same way as the Germans – by printing money. From an exchange rate of 2000 to the pound sterling in May 1921, the Austrian krone fell to 35,000 in May 1922, 52,000 in June and 350,000 in August. By then collapse was imminent, with potentially disastrous results.

Anyone living on fixed-interest investments or on a pension was cleaned out and became a virtual pauper. This category included many army officers and civil servants, who formed highly nationalistic and violently anti-semitic secret societies. As cash became worthless, everyone hoarded. Farmers in particular refused paper notes, which rapidly became worthless. Food riots started in the cities, forcing the authorities to hand out even more subsidies. Unemployment rose rapidly, and the unrest was further fuelled by communist agitation. Apart from the speculators, the people who fared best were those unionized workers who were able to muscle their way into indexed wage deals.

At last in August 1933 the Chancellor, Dr Ignaz Seipel, appealed to the League of Nations for help to stop the country from disintegrating. Britain, France, Italy and Czechoslovakia, among others, guaranteed a loan of 650 million gold kronen on the condition that they had a hand in putting the finances to rights. What they found, on closer investigation, was a horrific mixture of socialist benevolence and political expedience.

There were more state employees in Vienna to serve a republic of 6.5 million than there had been to serve the old Habsburg monarchy of 50 million. The state industries, and the railways in particular, typified the situation. Three men were employed for every mile of track, compared with two in Switzerland. The employees were union backed, so they received indexed payments. Rail fares were not indexed, however, and were only one-fifth of the level they should have been. Apart from the support needed for the railways, other subsidies were rife. Cigars were being sold in state stores at prices below their actual production cost.

By November 1922, however, the results of stabilizing efforts were becoming clear both at home and abroad; stability and confidence improved, and although there were serious withdrawal symptoms the country started to attract outside investment once again.

MEANWHILE, BACK IN GERMANY . . .

Despite a 10 per cent increase in banknotes issued in the first ten days of September 1922, those who were able and had the cash were now starting to exploit the situation. Many lived in the country with access to things of real value. It was a period, the complaint went, when brains counted for very little; those who survived well had guile and muscle. It was unwise to hold cash despite interest rates of 25 per cent per month. The soundest investment was to buy assets, such as a quantity of wheat, yards of timber or a herd of cattle, and then sell weeks later at an enormous profit. One quite sensible ploy was to take out a land mortgage and trade assets to pay off the loan in marks that had greatly declined in value.

Townspeople were not so lucky, particularly those on fixed incomes or pensions. Money was in short supply, so some authorities were allowed to issue their own currencies – called *Notgeld* – redeemable in marks after several months. Many new currency denominations were created. In Oldenberg, for example, the state bank issued 'Rye Bills', or *Roggenmarks*, secured on 125-kg lots of rye. The bills could be used as currency or redeemed in 1927 for 150 kg of rye (which included 25 kg 'interest'). Bartering systems were widespread. Many firms gave part-payments in coupons to be cashed in local shops. Metal theft became a major problem. Everything was fair game, including public monuments, brass door plates and knockers and lead roofs from churches.

Groups of foreign-exchange speculators called *winkelbankiers* were formed in many back alleys. On 1 January 1923, for example, a currency speculator could borrow enough paper marks (about 1980 million) to buy $100,000. On 1 April $80,000 could be sold to repay the bank, and a new loan raised, and then the process repeated. By the end of May the profit would have been $250,000 – provided it was kept in dollars.

Food was in short supply, since farmers refused to use depleted paper money as a means of exchange. A headmaster reported that 25 per cent of pupils leaving school were below average in weight and height, and 30 per cent were not fit for work. Professional people such as teachers and academics had a particularly hard time on their fixed salaries and lacked the muscle to negotiate indexed increases. Fee-earning doctors and lawyers were somewhat better off.

In industry itself, the situation remained relatively stable prior to the French occupation of the Rhineland. There were alarming developments none the less, particularly from the perspective of government and employees. Industrialists were able to sell very cheaply abroad, since the mark was worth so little in terms of foreign currency. But as these profits were made outside Germany, they were all too often kept there and very little contribution made it into the government's coffers.

Employers conducted regular wage deals with their employees, but income seldom kept up with prices. From 1913 to the end of 1922, for example, prices rose 1500 times and salaries only 200 times. Wages, originally paid weekly, were in the end paid twice a day, so rapid was the rise in inflation. Industrial shares rose well in nominal (mark) terms but collapsed in real value to 10 per cent of their pre-war level. By August 1922, the total stock-market capitalization was only equivalent to £200 million, and the authorities feared that large holdings in the major industries would be bought by foreigners.

Then in January 1923, after declaring Germany in breach of its reparations obligations, France occupied the industrial heartland of the country – the Rhineland. This confiscation of its major source of coal, iron and steel devastated the German industrial economy, particularly as equivalent materials now had to be imported. The French occupation imposed huge additional strains on the German government, but it also was to help unify a country that was rapidly disintegrating. It was agreed immediately that the Rhineland inhabitants would start a civil resistance campaign, supported by the German state. Operation of blast furnaces, steel mills, trains and boat transport was curtailed, affecting not only the occupiers but also neighbouring countries like Holland and Belgium.

The occupation made the budget imbalance even worse, and by March 1923 the German government's income represented only 30 per cent of its outgoings. Organizing taxation was a nightmare – an assessment made one week would be worth only half the amount a few weeks later. Of course, these weekly levies came mainly from the hourly paid; the rich, with their annual assessments, came off much better.

Matters then disintegrated quickly as the year progressed. Reichsbank chairman Dr Rudolph Havenstein announced with some pride that the bank was keeping 30 paper mills, 150 print works and 2000 printing presses working flat out producing notes. In the week beginning 17 August, 20,000 billion marks were being printed every day with outstanding efficiency. The following week 46,000 billion marks a day came off the presses and 63,000 billion the week after that. A few days' print run of notes was equivalent to two-thirds of all the marks already in circulation. It was a time when shoppers carried around their cash in mail sacks, baby carriages and wheelbarrows. It was said it took a wheelbarrowload of marks to buy a cabbage.

The social consequences were horrendous. Communist and fascists organized riots and demonstrations in Pomerania, East Prussia and Bavaria. Shops and warehouses were looted, and country people increasingly refused to take marks for produce. Barter was widespread. As at the time of the French Revolution, those found hoarding or delaying the distribution of food, speculating in money or preventing tax payments were penalized – not with the guillotine but with a month's jail and an unlimited fine. In the end, the strains led to the breakdown of civil administration and the declaration of martial law.

By the autumn of 1923 five million people were out of work, and many were suffering malnutrition. Government expenditure had risen to 1000 times its income, and the federation was breaking up. On 7 November, Adolf Hitler condemned the Versailles Treaty, the Jews and the communists and took advantage of the chaos in Bavaria to overthrow the Bavarian government in an attempted coup or *putsch*. It collapsed at the first whiff of musketry, and the future Führer was locked up in prison. There were riots and demands for secession in other states – Saxony, Prussia and Rhineland.

It was not a politician but a banker who had the solution to Germany's immediate problems. He was Dr Hjalmar Schacht, president of the Boden Credit Bank, who had given a lot of thought to the possibility of an asset-backed currency. Indeed, one had already been issued in the shape of the rye-backed *Roggenmark*. Schacht lobbied for a *Rentenmark* to be underwritten by guarantees on mortgages, landed property, industrial bonds, bank and commercial assets. Fortunately Dr Hans Luther, then minister of finance, learned about Schacht's proposal, and Schacht was made Commissioner of Currency in November 1924.

His plan was to issue *Rentenmarks*, each equivalent to one gold mark and one trillion (that is, one million billion) of the existing paper marks; the old money was convertible at that rate but not into gold or the underlying security. The initial issue was 500 million, but by July the following year it had expanded to 1800 million. Schacht insisted that the foreign currency in circulation and *Notgeld*, the private circulation, be converted into *Rentenmarks* or the latter would become worthless.

Incredibly, the plan worked, because it commanded confidence. The douche of freezing water stopped the frenzied note printing in its tracks – the unissued notes, it was estimated, would have filled 300 ten-ton railway wagons. The velocity of currency circulation declined markedly, and the mark stabilized on the foreign exchanges. The impact on the food supplies was felt almost immediately. Farmers now had the confidence to release food from their bulging granaries, the abattoirs increased their output, and the quantity of imported produce increased. Many speculators who had bargained on the continued fall in the mark were wiped out, obliged to redeem their foreign-currency positions in revalued marks.

As often happens, stabilizing the government's finances caused the greatest distress. The swollen bureaucracy was severely pruned. Civil servants had to work a nine-hour day, and their salaries were reduced. The numbers employed on the railway were decimated, and tariffs raised. Taxation and other government revenue, such as customs charges, was revalued, and by March 1925 the budget was balanced.

Dr Schacht, the man who had made it all happen, was made president of the Reichsbank for life. He seems to have been an unassuming but hugely industrious individual. There was something mole-like about him and appropriately – if oddly, for a man who saved his country's bacon – his office in the finance ministry had previously been a charwoman's cupboard. In Adam Fergusson's book, *When Money Dies*, Schacht's secretary, Fraulein Sreffeck, described how he worked:

> He sat on his chair and smoked in his little dark room, which still smelled of floor cloths. Did he read letters? No, he read no letters. Did he write letters? He wrote no letters. He telephoned in every direction and to every German or foreign place that had anything to do with money and foreign exchange as well as to the Reichsbank and the finance minister. And he smoked. We did not eat much during that time. We usually went home late, often by the last suburban train,

travelling third class. Apart from that he did nothing.

The withdrawal symptoms were horrendous. They could only have been accepted by a disciplined society, but they left terrible wounds, which greatly contributed to Hitler's rise to power. Many hundreds of thousands of the middle classes who depended upon state income or pensions were pauperized. The savings and livelihood of non-unionized working classes such as craftsmen, tradesmen and domestic servants were wiped out.

Wiped out too were those unlucky creditors holding mark-denominated bonds, whether they were loyal Germans buying War Loan or foreign bond holders. The collapse effectively destroyed the internal and external bond markets, which made it impossible for the government to raise foreign loans other than on very short terms. It was in part this absence of a bond market that caused Germany's repudiation of foreign debt in July 1931 after huge current-account withdrawals. This in turn caused Britain to go off the gold standard and triggered the American banking crisis in the same year.

Money, having been absurdly abundant, now became in very short supply and Schacht kept interest rates positive to avoid the disappearance of foreign currency. The first people to leave the scene were the speculators, who transferred their attention to trading the franc in Paris. Next to go were the racketeers who had bribed their way into the upper reaches of the civil service and the government – they brought down many of their collaborators with them. Finally, the empires built on paper by entrepreneurs and industrialists like Hugo Stinnes collapsed from excessive debt, leaving desperate unemployment behind them.

Massive resentment was felt by the vast majority of the population towards all those who had become rich at their expense. Those canny enough to trade in times of inflation and then

lend money at exorbitant interest rates during the following deflation were despised by those made destitute. Those benefiting were
corrupted by greed, dishonour and selfishness; the victims became resentful, xenophobic and anti-semitic, forming secret
societies. In times of real difficulty, it was found that the working
classes had taken to theft and prostitution, the middle class to
fraud, graft, bribery and corruption. And, as in the early four-
teenth century, those infected by the plague blamed those who had
escaped.

Business learned some lessons still worthy of attention.
Companies that had refrained from expansion or from vertical
integration did much better than those that had expanded hugely
on debt. While Stinnes failed, steelmakers like Krupp, Thyssen
and Gelsenkirchen survived. Deflation put a huge pressure on
costs. The *Rentenmark* stabilization, like the return of sterling to
the gold standard in 1925 and the French deflation of the early
1930s, effectively squeezed inflation from the economy.

SIX

THE TAMING OF GOVERNMENT

S o what exactly should governments be doing at this dangerous point in the economic cycle? There are now very few countries that could afford to spend their way out of trouble on the scale that is going to be needed, as the United States did in the early 1930s. Even Germany is suffering inflationary pressures after absorbing the eastern states and now expects zero growth in western Germany during 1993 – illustrating present constraints on even a strong economy. Some countries will try, initially, to maintain previous spending levels, hoping that the recession will follow post-war patterns; they are unlikely to succeed. What they should be doing is working on contingency plans to meet a financial crisis followed by a depression on the scale of the 1930s.

In so doing, they should bear one very important thing in mind. As the Americans showed in the early 1920s, and the British in the 1930s, it is not governments that lead countries out of a deep recession but entrepreneurs starting new industries and taking risks others will not accept. To flourish, these people need a stable economy, an advantageous tax system and low rates of interest; none of these can be had if the government attempts to maintain its own spending at the expense of the achievers. The entrepreneurs will simply take their ideas and energy and move elsewhere.

If this is to be avoided, it means cutting back the power of government, which will not be easy given the number of people who will expect the politicians to come to the rescue. But this will have to happen. As the central power declines, and as large public and private corporations become like stranded whales, which have to be broken up, we are likely to see a growth in individual independence almost without precedence.

The history of previous depressions suggests that where a government (like the United Kingdom, but unlike the United States) is not itself drastically in debt, it should plan three fundamental measures: to balance the budget, to provide support for the unemployed (see chapter 7), to underwrite a certain amount of private credit and to support housing (see chapter 8).

BOILING DOWN THE BUDGET

The scale of public spending in most western countries is so large that any cutbacks in expenditure will require painful decisions, particularly as the amount of money available to spend from tax revenues will inevitably shrink. If central government declines as it did in the United States and France in the early 1930s, by 1994 government income will have fallen by around one-third from its level in 1990. This fall should be matched by proportionate spending reductions. The necessary shift in thinking will need a strength of imagination and application that has been shown by few present-day politicians, but this is how a contingency plan might apply to Britain.

The total expenditure of UK central government in 1990 was £198 billion. The biggest single sum went on social-security benefits (£49 billion). Other significant items were grants to local authorities (£38 billion), health (£26 billion), defence (£22 billion) and debt interest (£18 billion), together representing some 77 per cent of the total. Various subsidies to housing, nationalized industries, farming, transport and the like cost the taxpayer £5.5 billion.

This huge spending machine grew nearly 2.5 times in nominal terms during the 1980s. Among other things, it accounted for 428,000 public servants by 1989. The largest departmental employers were Defence (141,000), the Chancellor's department (109,000), Employment (55,000), Environment (31,000), Home Office (41,000) and Health and Social Services (now split, but totalling 94,000). This does not include those employed by local government, which again represents a big fixed cost to the community.

A decline of government income of, say, one-third would imply a state spending fall of £66 billion from the levels above, or £22 billion a year – the total defence budget in 1990. Clearly, any fall in spending should mean at least a corresponding decline in public-service employment – a pro rata decline of 142,000 in the civil departments but many more in local government. These reductions will not be achieved unless the government is led by clear-sighted individuals prepared to be extremely unpopular. They will have to cut through forty years of accepted practices by thinking of new ways to privatize services, reduce bureaucratic costs, enforce savings and transfer the cost of paying for public services to those who can afford it.

The situation faced by the new president of the United States is rather more formidable. Declining tax revenues and increasing welfare payments have raised the planned budget deficit for 1992 to an all-time estimated record of $400 billion – or 6.7 per cent of

GNP, the highest since 1945. Despite cuts in interest rates, the economy has been growing sluggishly for three years while federal spending is up by 29 per cent since 1989. During fiscal 1991, spending increased by 11.5 per cent, while income rose only 2 per cent, so sharply augmenting the budget imbalance.

Although President Bill Clinton may see himself as a new Roosevelt, the US dollar is no longer backed by gold as it was in the 1930s, and it has lost 70 per cent of its purchasing power since the United States came off the gold standard in 1970. Although the government may well try to spend its way out of the recession, any spending initiatives on the scale of the New Deal would have a devastating impact on holders of US currency and securities.

Unlike the central government, most US states are obliged by law to balance their budgets, but they too are suffering from falling tax revenues and increased liabilities. California has slashed welfare payments by 25 per cent and curtailed other spending as its budget is squeezed between higher costs and falling revenue; there are already five welfare recipients for every six taxpayers, and high earners are moving elsewhere. In the north-east, Connecticut's credit rating has been downgraded because of its escalating debt, and there is strenuous public resistance to increased taxation to meet the projected deficit.

NEITHER A BORROWER . . .

If a government cannot balance its budget, it must borrow the difference between what it raises and what it spends – the bigger the deficit, the bigger the borrowing. Balanced budgets will be hard to achieve as income declines faster than spending. But it must be tackled if the government is not to suck in all the available funds at the expense of everybody else – what economists call 'crowding out the private sector'. There are various ways to reduce government borrowing requirements and at the same time create an environment that encourages entrepreneurship.

PRIVATIZE REMAINING PUBLIC INDUSTRIES

As described in chapter 5, it was the publicly owned railways in France, Germany and Austria that were responsible for much of the respective state deficits. In modern terms, this implies that Britain's remaining public industries should be privatized. Loss-making coal mines should be given to their workforce.

CREATE PRIVATE-SECTOR AGENCIES

Government should change fixed costs into variable costs wherever possible. Immediate steps should be taken to convert all the government executive services into private-sector agencies through which any remaining funds could be channelled. This could include departments such as the Inland Revenue or VAT offices. The remaining state employees would retain an important monitoring role. Steps have already been taken in the 1988 Local Government Act to introduce competition into local-government services (see chapter 10); this should now be extended to central government.

RETURN TO STABLE MONEY

Until it entered World War I (and subsequently from 1925 to 1931), Britain was on the gold standard, as was the United States until 1971. This was a system whereby the currencies were convertible into fixed amounts of gold. *Fiat*, or inconvertible, paper-money has never been successful in the long run. Particularly after a period of financial turmoil, a currency needs to be based on some form of collateral. The gold standard imposed an anti-inflationary discipline on politicians and central banks – if their policies caused the currencies to depreciate, foreign holders could exchange their holdings for gold.

The Grace Commission, appointed to investigate US government waste, warned in 1984 that rising federal debt could bankrupt the United States by 1995 and that stringent measures were needed to be taken to balance the budget (see chapter 4, p.43). Although the Commission did not mention a return to the gold standard, this could clearly reduce the chances of non-US holders of dollar securities forcing a run on the currency.

REDUCE GOVERNMENT WASTE

A commission to reduce government waste should be set up in the United Kingdom, along lines similar to the Grace Commission. In his book, *Bankruptcy 1995*, Harry Figgie describes how the commission identified 2478 cost-saving recommendations, which could have saved the federal government $424 billion over the three years to 1987. Though their report was never acted upon, these were some of the options suggested.

● Over 3500 defence installations (of a total of 4000) could be closed without endangering efficiency or effectiveness.

● A single accounting system should replace the 332 incompatible systems in use by different government agencies.

● Procurement procedures should be simplified – the process of buying a marine hammer, priced at $71, accumulated $365 in administration expenses.

● A host of old programmes should be reviewed and possibly terminated. One example was a rural electricity programme, started in 1935, that loaned $2 billion a year at reduced rates to help rural Americans buy generating equipment – although 99 per cent now have installed electricity. The programme incurred an annual loss of £350 million.

CUT PUBLIC-SERVICE PAY

As the depression continues many of those in the private sector – and the vast majority of the unemployed – will be obliged to take a cut in their living standards. The same rules should also apply to the public sector's salaries and pensions. In September 1931, the supplementary budget of the British national government cut public-sector salaries by 15 per cent.

REFORM INCOME TAX

To reduce administration costs, all those with incomes above a certain level should pay a flat rate of income tax. Capital gains tax should be abolished. Government must transfer some of the cost of public services such as health and education to those who can afford to pay for them. Those who cannot afford to pay should be subject to negative income tax – in other words, they should be granted compensatory tax allowances. This would cut out much of the bureaucracy associated with the present benefit or entitlement programmes.

PAYMENT FROM THOSE WHO CAN AFFORD IT

Moving from the general to the particular, there are ways in which individual functions within government can cut their costs. Notable among them are health and education. Those who can afford to pay for health and education should do so. This would not only reduce the direct cost to government but also eliminate much of the bureaucracy involved in collecting taxes and recycling them in the form of public services. In recent times, there have been several examples of reducing the cost of publicly provided health and education in this way. One comes from New Zealand, where a range of public services has been rationalized. Another can be found in the US state of Oregon, which has been forced to review the extent of free health care paid for with public money.

NEW ZEALAND SETS THE PACE

In 1990, the New Zealand government under prime minister and National party leader, Jim Bolger, introduced a radical cost-saving budget, masterminded by finance minister Ruth Richardson. In the *Financial Times* of 24 July 1990, she was quoted as follows: 'In general, those individuals and families with reasonable means should attend to their own needs. As a broad principle, the top one-third of all income earners can be expected to meet most of the cost of their social services.' When the government assumed office, it introduced a budget proposing to reduce public spending to 37.4 per cent of GDP by 1994–5; by contrast, the current British level is 41.7 per cent and is forecast to be 42.2 per cent by 1994–5. This is how New Zealand is taming government spending without destroying support for those who really need it.

Like Britain, New Zealand has a national health service – although unlike the British system, patients have always had to pay part of the charge for a consultation. Above-average earners will now have to pay the full price of NZ$30 (about £9) to visit a doctor as well as full prescription, dental and optical charges. In addition, around 20 per cent of the top-earning families – those with salaries of NZ$32,500 (£10,000) or more – will have to pay up to NZ$50 (£15) a night as a contribution to their hospital costs (up to a total of NZ$500, or £150, a year). Anybody wanting non-core services like cosmetic surgery has to pay the full cost.

As in Britain, the market concept of suppliers and purchasers has been introduced to the New Zealand health service, whereby practitioners in four regional health authorities buy services from some twenty-five Crown Health Enterprises, which manage the hospitals. In all, it is estimated that 23 per cent of state health spending will be privately funded, up from 11 per cent in 1980.

In the sphere of education, school governors are now being given control over their budgetary spending, and the more enterprising are offering fee-earning services and charging full rates for overseas students. On the principle that a college education will lead to higher earnings and that nearly 75 per cent of students come from families above the income level of NZ$32,500, the full cost of maintenance will be borne privately. Students will be required to pay 10 per cent of their fees, the balance being progressively funded by loans.

Social welfare is also affected. In 1991, unemployment benefit was cut by 10 per cent. It is no longer payable to those aged below 18 and only at a reduced rate to those under 25. Those over the retirement age of 65 will have to pay a surcharge on income tax of 25 per cent (making the top marginal rate 57 per cent) as a contribution to their pension.

SHORTLISTING IN OREGON

The New Zealand system has shown what can be done by charging for services, but this will probably not be enough to reduce the burden of cost. As with other national or regional schemes, the state of Oregon found it could not afford to offer a full range of free treatments and has taken steps to cut down the number of benefits available to the 226,000 people on the state Medicare programme.

A group of five doctors, a social worker and a nurse ranked the 709 treatments provided by the state according to risk; appendectomies were high on the list, as was maternity care. Bottom of the list came conditions that did not threaten lifespan or the quality of life. The state now pays for 587 treatments but reserves the right to review the list if cash runs short.

UNWINDING BRITISH BUREAUCRACY

In Britain the health service has already begun to be prised away from central and local government control, although the system is still largely paid for out of taxed income. The next stage is for newly independent hospital trusts and general practices to come together in a system of Health Maintenance Organizations (HMOs), which compete to attract health-care needs. HMOs have not been all that economically successful in the United States, where too much of the finance came from company-funded pro-grammes, but they could become much more competitive if the choice of which one to use is made by individuals paying insurance premiums from their own pockets.

Everyone would be required to pay a basic health-insurance premium, with those below a certain income and those with special needs given a tax allowance or credit. Anyone wishing to pay more than the standard charge should top up their insurance payments out of taxed income. Unwinding the central bureaucracy is starting to work. Already hospital trusts are finding that they can provide a better service specializing in a certain range of treatments at a lower cost. But they will have to prune much further to reach the efficiency of some Japanese hospitals that have one-third of the number of auxiliaries and administrators than is usual in Britain.

The Conservative administration has also started to unwind education from direct central and local government control with encouraging results. Once headmasters learn to run their schools through bursars, like the private sector, they will be able to use their funds in a way that attracts parents. Those who can afford it will pay the cost, and for others a tax allowable insurance system will pay for basic 'vouchers' that may be cashed at a school of the recipient's choice. If parents wish to pay more, then this should come out of taxed income. Once schools become independent, most of the state and local overheads can be eliminated except for the cost of monitoring standards.

HELP FOR SMALLER COMPANIES

Apart from a balanced budget, support for the unemployed and a certain amount of underwriting of housing debt are the other two important areas that must be addressed by government. Both are discussed in later chapters. A wide range of special needs will have to be attended to as the recession deepens. One business sector that will be in particular need of help is the small business.

In the first half of 1992 British clearing banks reportedly had £45 billion in outstanding loans to the small business sector (defined as having sales of £1 million or less), the loans being heavily skewed towards the very small concerns. Company liquidations in 1991 meant that 2.2 per cent of the total loan book had to be written off, up from a previous peak of 1.8 per cent in the 1980s. During the depression, it is estimated that some 20 per cent, or £9 billion, will need to be written off.

One of the most pressing difficulties for otherwise viable small firms is late payment from customers. Trade Indemnity, the UK's premier debt insurance house, reports that average payments for small companies were received 31 days after the due date compared with 26 days for larger concerns, and the figure deteriorated in the second quarter of 1992. Late payments were worst in textiles, food services, builders merchants and steel stockholders, but many others were not far behind. It is stupid, not to mention unethical, for large companies to take advantage of their financial muscle to force small suppliers into liquidation through late payment; these are the very subcontractors that will be needed when the larger concerns are forced to slim down operations – see chapter 10. Two measures need to be considered by the government. One would make it easier for small companies to get refinancing, while the other would allow some of their outstanding loans to be underwritten.

BETTER BES AND LOAN GUARANTEES

The government could help to rescue basically sound small businesses that might otherwise fail through a major default such as a bad debt. Instead of the clearing banks having to take most of the risk, enterprises could benefit from an extension of the Business Expansion Scheme (BES), which would allow tax relief for outside shareholders involved in a debt for equity swap.

In the early 1980s, the Chancellor introduced the BES to give tax relief for investments into new small companies providing they observed certain rules: the businesses had to be a new venture approved by the Inland Revenue; each participant was allowed 5 per cent or less of the equity (which had to be kept for five years); and the shareholder could not draw a salary. As expected, many of the ventures failed, but a large number survived, and the ability to attract equity from shareholders meant that these companies raised less debt.

The present BES programme ends in fiscal 1992. However, it still has considerable merit as a vehicle for attracting outside shareholders into basically solvent small businesses put at risk by another's failure or late payments. Should the clearing bank be able to persuade the current shareholders that an injection of capital were an alternative to closure, many businesses might be saved.

Where equity participation was not appropriate, the Small Firms Loan Guarantee Scheme (SFLGS) might be extended to existing businesses where the government was willing to guarantee a proportion of the loan, so encouraging the bank not to call in its debt. The SFLGS was introduced in the early 1980s to encourage the formation of businesses where neither equity finance or loan guarantees could be provided. Where a proposition meets the criteria, the Department of Trade and Industry is prepared to guarantee at least 50 per cent of loans between £15,001 and £100,000 (up to 85 per cent where the business is in an inner-city zone). A separate Small Firms Loan Arrangement exists for loans from £1000 to £15,000.

HAVE OUR GOVERNMENTS LEARNED FROM THE 1930s?

By the autumn of 1992, there was little sign that the British administration had learned much from the National Government of 1931 – or the American New Deal. The party in power seems to be battling against rising nationalism in order to conclude a federal treaty in Europe, while their fellow countrymen would prefer to see their politicians engaged nearer home. There is little talk of the really serious problems of the depression and how to cope with them, such as underwriting home ownership or small businesses, introducing a comprehensive programme for the unemployed (or those wanting to set up on their own) or drastically reducing the size and scope of the government.

Failure to implement these measures could mean disaster for the private wealth of the people of Britain. Merchant bankers Morgan Grenfell have conducted a study of personal assets in Britain. They concluded that, at the end of 1991, residential buildings, life-assurance policies and pension funds represented two-thirds of people's assets. If anything resembling scenario 3 occurs, as discussed in chapter 5 (and President Clinton's programme might well accelerate it), a decline of 50 per cent in property and financial markets – let alone other assets – could cause the net wealth of the personal sector to decline by 35 per cent. Luckily for Britain, the gross public debt in relation to output, unlike that of the United States, is lower than that of its major competitors, and interest absorbed only around 10 per cent of the state's income in 1992 compared to 20 per cent in the USA.

President Bill Clinton's policy does take some cues from the New Deal, such as an annual $20 billion earmarked for public works and $60 billion over four years for education and training. Funding for employee training is proposed to come from a 1.5 per cent levy on the payroll which, ironically, might accelerate unemployment as more companies seek to reduce their liability. But all this big government spending seems to be aimed at supporting existing industries, not encouraging entrepreneurs to create industries for the future.

SEVEN

GETTING BRITAIN TO WORK

Many of those put out of work during the Great Depression of the 1990s will not again find regular jobs when it finally ends. The easy days of paid employment during the 1980s ended when public and private organizations, forced to slim down, realized they could operate quite effectively with many fewer people. Even before the nineties' depression, there were some private estimates that, by 1995, 50 per cent of the working population would be working either for themselves or in small independent groups. This will only add to the pressures on employment as the economy comes out of the slump – at which point unemployment may reach 5.5 million.

Mass unemployment could not come at a worse time. Central and local governments will be having to make their own savings as their income from taxation falls. This will reduce still further the amount available to expand public expenditure – just when many would like to see it raised to help the unemployed. This is not just a question for government ministers. It deeply affects all taxpayers asked to pay more for unemployment benefit. The tolerance threshold in this regard was reached in California in 1991, when governor Pete Wilson was faced with a tax revolt. California's six taxpayers to every five welfare recipients refused to increase their contributions, and welfare entitlements had to be cut by 25 per cent. In a deep depression the balance will tip even further.

However, merely cutting benefits is no solution. Most unemployed people would far rather work than remain idle, provided the activity was useful, and they were not just treated as cheap labour. New ideas are needed to combine useful work with training. If this is not done, many already disadvantaged people now existing in inner cities on drugs and crime will become more violent should their state subsidies be cut. Even normally law-abiding citizens could find it easier to steal or commit fraud than take an unremunerative job. The numbers will be considerable. Even if 2.5 million new self-employed jobs could be created over a five-year period, nearly double that figure could remain out of work, putting a huge strain upon the public purse. This would force a responsible government to raise taxes and to come up with a plan that would both help those out of work and satisfy taxpayers that their money was being well spent.

One solution would be to offer a choice to those able to work and signing on for unemployment benefit. They can either be given help to set up on their own or opportunities to work on public projects. Training would be provided in either case. Those who chose to do neither would be paid nothing. This is a perfectly viable proposition, particularly if the majority of projects and, perhaps, the funding are based firmly within the community. What follows draws upon job-creating measures that have worked in the past and suggests how these might operate in today's climate.

In the 1930s one of the few effective work-creation programmes was the Civilian Conservation Corps initiated by US
President Roosevelt as part of the New Deal. The programme was
very successful and showed the need for four essential components: the work must be worthwhile; there should be a strong
element of training; the programme must be well led and administered; and, where possible, the work should be community-
based. Such a programme could work in contemporary Britain.
Several voluntary organizations already exist as models and, possibly, as frameworks, and there is plenty of useful work to be done.
There is also an existing structure for organizing those who may be
resentful of direction and will need particular supervision and
control. And it is possible, as will be shown, to manage a job-
creation programme at minimum cost to the public purse.

DOLE QUEUES

The scale of unemployment in Britain is likely to be in excess of
anything that was experienced in the 1930s. Then, in 1932, it rose
to a peak of nearly 15 per cent, hitting hardest those staple
northern industries such as coalmining, iron and steel, shipbuild-
ing and textiles. Those who lived in the Midlands and the South
fared rather better. During the 1930s a whole range of new
industries blossomed, such as motor vehicles, domestic appliances, aircraft, radio and construction, demonstrating how the
spirit of initiative can flourish in times of depression.

In the 1990s the problems will be much more acute. Chapter
10 describes how technology and new working practices will
enable organizations to run on substantially reduced nummbers of
permanent employees, by contracting out services previously
provided in-house. Some will find the process not all that painful –
they will be able to set up on their own immediately, providing

services that duplicate their erstwhile full-time jobs. Those who fare worst will be middle managers with only executive skills, and untrained people who rely mainly on their muscle for getting work.

The shock will be unsettling for those who took it for granted that the welfare state would look after them whatever happened. There was no culture of encouragement for people to take responsibility for their own lives or feel that they had duties as well as rights. Many will become resentful and possibly violent. This is all the more reason why any proposal to deal with rising unemployment should provide worthwhile, paid work with an element of training.

The community was the bedrock for the first English unemployment programmes, introduced during the extremely hard times of the 1590s, when the local community was given responsibility for looking after those without work. This functioned well until the equally difficult 1830s and 1840s, when the local cost became too great. As is often the case, the national solutions that followed did not serve local needs, and the results were disastrous. The exceptions to this rule have been a handful of US programmes introduced as part of Roosevelt's New Deal, such as the Civil Works Administration and the Civilian Conservation Corps discussed in chapter 5.

NOT EXACTLY A NEW PROBLEM

The first Poor Laws were enacted in England during 1597–8 and 1601. These were particularly difficult times in the middle of the 'Little Ice Age' when there were regular crop failures, and those who could not make a living had the option of either starving or working cooperatively with others. The laws were known as the Acts of Confinement and required the local poor to work with others within, and supported by, the community. These problems were not confined to England, and in many areas of Europe similar programmes saved countless lives.

The funding came from a Poor Rate levied from members of the parish, and those without support were encouraged to work cooperatively either 'indoors' in a workhouse or 'outdoors', from their own homes. Under the Act of 1601, churchwardens and other substantial property owners were appointed overseers to provide work for the rural poor, with the duty to apprentice pauper children. In the towns, paid overseers were appointed to perform a similar function.

During the nineteenth century, in the difficult times which led up to the Hungry Forties, there was national alarm that too much was being spent on poor relief. Following a Royal Commission, the Poor Law Amendment Act was passed in 1834. The new act was draconian. It denied relief to those able to work 'outside' and granted support only to workhouse inmates who had to pass a 'workhouse test'. This spartan regime succeeded in reducing the official percentage of the unemployed population from 8.8 per cent in 1834 to 4.3 per cent in 1860 – but at terrible human cost. Much later, in 1911, the first true state National Insurance Act was passed, providing unemployed people with support levied by contributions from the state, the employer and the employee.

LOOKING FOR WORK? PROVE IT

Different countries have approached unemployment in different ways. In the United States, David Stockman, Reagan's budget director in the early 1980s, observed:

I just don't accept the assumption that the federal government has a responsibility to supplement the income of the working poor through a whole series of transfer payments. We believe that the guy who takes two jobs and makes $26,000 a year shouldn't be obligated to transfer part of his income and taxes to the guy who's making $10,000.

In 1981, the Reagan Administration passed the Omnibus Reconciliation Act, which made it mandatory for work to be done in exchange for state support. Under 'workfare', as this system became known, anyone applying for benefit has to prove they are actively seeking work before any payment is made. If the search for a job still fails, the able-bodied recipient must work in community projects run by public and private non-profit-making agencies. He or she is offered the alternative of learning a new skill.

The danger of workfare, as it is administered in states like West Virginia, is that the work offered is generally of low grade, and no training is given. Recipients are required to do jobs like police helpers, ambulance assistants, library and park aides, clerical workers and labourers. These are all necessary jobs, but those obliged to do them feel they are a form of cheap labour. Massachusetts has a more imaginative programme, which places the emphasis on job training and work opportunity.

In California, applicants for benefit are given a simple test to evaluate their education aptitude. If they fall below a certain level they are sent back to school for remedial courses in maths, reading and writing to secondary-school equivalent levels. After the course, individuals are given a week-long course in how to apply for jobs and how best to present themselves at an interview. The reports of this initiative are excellent, and the spirit of mutual self-help operates as a powerful motivation.

In Switzerland, which has almost the lowest unemployment rate in Europe, compulsory unemployment insurance was introduced in 1977. Those applying for support receive benefits related to previous income levels, which is available for only eight months from application. No person under 20 can receive payment. In Scandinavia, Sweden has a private insurance system. The unemployment societies are licensed by the government to provide members with benefits from contributions provided equally by employers, employees and the state.

BETTER BRITISH BENEFIT – OR UB93

At present there is no obligation for anyone drawing unemployment benefit in Britain to give anything in return apart from assurances that they receive no income, have limited or no savings and are looking for work. In a paper called *Why Not Work?*, Ralph Howell, Conservative MP for an East Anglian constituency, points out the huge disadvantages of this policy. It costs an enormous amount to administer, the taxpaying community receives nothing in return, and vast numbers of people (particularly in a recession) progressively lose the hope and the capacity to work. It also creates a poverty trap in which taking a low-paid job can leave a person worse off than staying on benefit. Howell estimates that, under the present system, the annual cost of providing unemployment benefit is some £20 billion (or 10 per cent of the total UK national budget in 1990), made up as follows.

THE BURDEN OF BENEFIT: 1990–91

PROGRAMME	COST (£bn)
UNEMPLOYMENT BENEFIT	0.8
INCOME SUPPORT	8.5
COMMUNITY-CHARGE BENEFIT	2.2
ONE-PARENT BENEFIT	0.2
FAMILY CREDIT	0.5
HOUSING BENEFIT	4.4
ADMINISTRATION	3.1
TOTAL	**19.7**

Howell proposes to pay all able-bodied individuals unable to find work a tax-free salary of £100 in exchange for a full working week. They would work on conservation projects, supervised by individuals paid an additional £25 per week. Under-20s would get two-thirds of the full rate. Those declining to work would be paid nothing. Should the plan be adopted, and assuming all 2.4 million unemployed (the figure on which Howell based his calculations – it has since risen) took up the offer, Howell believes that the administration could be reduced both locally and centrally with the following result.

MAKING BENEFIT PAY

ALLOCATION SOURCE	COST (£bn)
2.25 MILLION @ £100 PER WEEK	11.7
150,000 UNDER-20s @ £66.66 PER WEEK	0.5
240,000 SUPERVISORS @ £125 PER WEEK	0.3
LOCAL ADMINISTRATION	2.4
CENTRAL ADMINSTRATION	0.1
TOTAL	15.0

Howell claims the following benefits would flow from his proposal.

● The participants would be better off not only financially but also in terms of self-confidence and future employment prospects.

● Many of those now claiming benefit also work in the 'black economy'. Howell's plan would reduce fraudulent payments.

● Those tempted to take a 'breather' between jobs would either work or be paid nothing.

● Those disabled or only able to work part-time would be paid pro rata for their time.

● Single mothers would be helped by the programme with their children left in day-centres staffed largely by suitably trained recipients of workfare payments.

· CIVILIAN CONSERVATION CORPS ·
A WORKING MODEL

But what about the work itself? The scale of the likely unemployment problem calls for a much more extensive work programme than is at present available in any country and would require a considerable feat of organization. Yet it has been done before. On 21 March 1933, only days after his inauguration, US President Franklin D. Roosevelt addressed Congress and announced:

I propose to create a Civilian Conservation Corps that would be used in simple work, not interfering with normal employment and confining itself to forestry, the prevention of soil erosion, flood control, and similar projects.

More important, however, than the material gains will be the moral and spiritual value of such work. The Americans who are now walking the streets and receiving private and public relief would infinitely prefer to work. We can take a vast army of unemployed out into healthful surroundings. We can eliminate to some extent at least the threat that enforced idleness brings to spiritual and moral stability.

It is not a panacea for all the unemployment, but it is an essential step in this emergency. . . . I estimate that 250,000 men can be given temporary employment by the early summer if you will give me the authority to proceed within the next two weeks.

Congress approved the plan on 31 March. Instead of creating a new ministry, the President used the existing War, Interior, Agricultural and Labor Departments to generate the essential elements of the project, under the direction of Robert Fechner, a Boston labour leader. Whatever their criticism of other parts of the New Deal legislation, most commentators have high praise for the CCC and its achievements. It took a proportion of young men away from the despair of unemployment and gave them creative employment and training in practical skills, which they might otherwise have never experienced. It also provided many with leadership and initiative training, which served their country well when it entered World War II.

Between 1933 and 1938 more than two million men participated in the programme; at its height, 502,000 enrollees were organized in over 2500 camps. The average age of those enlisted was between 18 and 19, after they had completed eight years of schooling. The average cost for an enrollee was $1000 in 1940, including clothing, keep and an allotment to dependants. Between them the enrollees cleared 68,000 miles of firebreaks and 814,000 acres of woodland, hacked out 13,100 miles of trails and planted more than 100 million trees, in addition to numerous other accomplishments.

The CCC was an all volunteer corps, which took only young men between the ages of 18 and 25 who were unmarried and came from a family on welfare relief. Initially, only one in five volunteers applying to the local state-relief organization was selected. After an interview and medical check the candidate had to sign an Oath of Enrollment, which required him to work for six months in a camp away from home, with two short periods of leave. The pay of $30 a month was not exactly generous, but it was pure pocket money, $22–$25 of which had to be sent home for the family. The six-month term could be renewed three times providing work was satisfactory, and at the end the enrollee was given a scroll confirming an honorable discharge. The contract was broken if a man were away for two days without leave.

Enrollees were first sent to a 'conditioning' army base where they were provided with a working uniform and brought into a suitable physical (and probably mental) state for work. This was essential because the depression had left many families unable to support their children, who were consequently often underweight, undernourished and unfit for work. Once in better health, they moved to camps near the work project.

The War Department ran these camps with active and reserve officers and men. By July 1933, nearly 4500 naval, army and marine officers had been appointed and, although not under military discipline, the enrollees were obliged under their Oath of Enrollment to obey a brisk camp routine. They rose at 6 a.m. and, after breakfast, started on the day's project. Work continued until 4 p.m. with half an hour's break for lunch before returning to camp. After the Retreat ceremony, the flag was lowered, and there was an inspection followed by dinner. The enrollees were then free until lights out at 10 p.m.

A camp usually housed a 'company' of 200 men under the control of a commander, a junior officer and a project superintendent. The work was organized by the Local Experienced Men (LEM) – organizers, trainers and tradesmen who led the teams. Those who took extra responsibilities were rewarded with additional payments. Many of the camps were built by the enrollees – often from felled forest trees – and until these were ready, they lived in army tents.

Education became an important part of camp life, and an adviser was appointed to run a range of courses, usually after working hours. In time, ten hours each week could be set aside for general education and vocation training – many of the enrollees could not read or write. Other subjects included car mechanics, diesel engines, simple aeronautics, forestry, journalism and photography. These were supplemented by games, entertainment and other recreational activities.

Health and work safety were taken very seriously because almost all of the work was physical, and there were several fatalities as a result of rock slides, falling timber, fire fighting and drowning. Each camp had a doctor appointed from the area, and in due course everyone was given a first-aid course. The camp administration also insisted on cleanliness. Each enrollee had to bathe once a week and to clean his teeth every day; regular inspections ensured that the dormitories were kept clean and tidy, and that kit was kept washed and in good repair.

The majority of the camps were on national forest land, and the CCC did a wonderful job of helping to protect and manage woodlands. The work, mainly woodland clearing, tree planting, fire prevention and fire fighting was supervised by LEMs and foresters. These were older men who took charge of the gangs and trained them in the practical crafts of building look-out structures, dealing with fires, road and trail making, forestry, driving machinery and so on.

The Department of Agriculture ran a Soil Erosion Service to help farmers and ranchers use land and water resources so as to reduce loss from flood and erosion. In conjunction with this, many camps were set up in dust-bowl areas, with enrollees drawn from local farming communities. They did important work, planting trees, building gullies, repairing levees, tiling drains and helping to control the erosion of millions of acres of farmland that would otherwise have had to be abandoned.

Today's visitors to US national parks have cause to thank the CCC people who worked there in the 1930s, building roads, trails, look-out positions, picnic areas and sewerage systems. The corps was also used extensively for disaster relief. Enrollees built sand-bag dikes along the banks of the Mississippi and Ohio rivers in the great flood of 1937, helped to rescue flood victims and were involved in cleaning up after the water receded. After the New England Hurricane of 1938, which killed more than 500 people, the crews repaired damage to 14,000 homes and buildings. In addition, the CCC also built museums, cleaned up canals, built park railways and restored monuments. Later they helped to build airfields, before the programme was finally wound up in June 1942 when the United States involvement in World War II made unemployment a redundant issue.

A BRITISH FRAMEWORK EXISTS

If a similar enterprise were to be launched in Britain, the example of the CCC suggests three essential elements: a system for creating and classifying programmes; project organization and training; and supervision. As things stand, there are currently many voluntary organizations in Britain at work on the environment, and the two that have probably come up with the most working projects are British Trust for Conservation Volunteers (BTCV), which works primarily in the countryside, and Groundwork Trust (GT), which operates in more urban environments. The first project of the Conservation Corps (as the BTCV was then called) was to clear the scrub-covered slopes of Juniper Hill in Surrey in 1959. The corps was set up by the Council for Nature (now the Nature Conservancy Council) and its administration was first undertaken by the Royal Geographical Society.

Unfortunately, natural areas seldom stay attractive on their own. They need a great deal of attention, for which there is usually little money available. The corps founders understood this and believed that the work could be undertaken by enthusiastic volunteers. It was thought that many would be motivated by the idea of doing something tangible to preserve the countryside, and so it proved. Volunteers have come from school sixth forms, universities and the general public to make their varying contributions, lasting a day, a weekend or even a week. Canada and the USA have similar programmes.

Much of BTCV's work is in the countryside, although an increasing demand is coming from the inner cities, which is also a source of volunteers for rural work. In areas such as Snowdonia in North Wales, for example, there is no large pool of local volunteers, so help is needed from more populated areas. Increasingly, the Trust gets volunteers from among the unemployed who find a focus and a sense of fulfilment from contributing to and enjoying the countryside. Now, some 800 self-help community groups have been started in villages, towns and cities under the aegis of the BTCV. Such group activities could be suitable for working holidays, and they do valuable work in clearing derelict and dilapidated areas, removing rubbish from canals, creating nature trails and the like.

If unemployed people were put to work in expanded BTCV-type projects, there are a tremendous number of potential projects for them to tackle in Britain, such as the large areas of derelict woodland, which have not been managed since the war. Other areas of attention could be the national parks, nature reserves, local-authority country parks, and sites administered by the National Trust. Work on these would be similar to CCC projects, and it should be possible to introduce wider training in a variety of skills as part of the remit.

In Britain, BTCV is going strong. In 1992 it planned about 600 week-long projects, with an additional 60-odd run by its Scottish branch. It has a network of some 200 staff around the country who are called in by potential clients. These may be private landowners, for example the National Trust or local authorities, who work very closely with the volunteers. The field officer surveys the job to assess whether it is suitable for volunteers – BTCV generally confines itself to work that would not otherwise be handled by contractors. Then again, some projects may need heavy equipment, in which case BTCV volunteers may work as part of a larger project involving contractors organized by the client. Once the project has been agreed, it goes into the local and head-office schedule.

The local field officers have their own resources, such as transport and tools, and make local arrangements for accommodation, catering and medical support – enough to sustain 12–14 adults away from home for six days. Recruitment is handled centrally from the Wallingford headquarters in Oxfordshire, which advertises nationally in conservancy magazines, public libraries and the like. The projects are tremendously varied. Members pay their own travel expenses and a weekly fee of around £35 for accommodation and food. Field officers generally organize accommodation for the teams in village halls where the better-provided have hot water, showers and kitchens. Some of the National Trust locations have their own lodges for volunteers. In return for the work, BTCV charges the client a fee of around £600 for the work done, depending on the number of working days and the ability to pay. Team work is organized by a project leader who has appropriate work experience and would typically direct fifteen people (leaders may well have started work as team members and taken additional training in leadership).

Although 6000 to 7000 volunteers are involved in the week-long projects, in the course of a year more than ten times that number work in local and community groups. The range of work is impressive. The majority of the projects are organized by local people to meet local needs and aspirations.

LOTS TO DO IN URBAN AREAS

The first Groundwork Trust project was started at St Helens and Knowsley, Lancashire, in 1980 to clear up and remodel areas of dereliction left by an earlier industrial age. The idea was to create local partnerships between the private, public and voluntary sectors. The structure was first mooted by the Countryside Commission and has since spread to many areas and counties that now have their own Groundwork Trusts, such as Merthyr Tydfil, Durham, the Colne Valley and Hertfordshire. In 1985, it was decided to set up a central group in Birmingham to back up local initiatives and to extend the number of Trusts to a government-set target of fifty.

It costs around £100,000 to set up a Trust. County or city councils usually start the ball rolling, getting extra funding from the appropriate Department of the Environment group and local business interests. Each Trust is self-contained, with its own board made up of the contributors. Most of the work is handled by contractors, but there is an important role for the community and voluntary sector. Each has a local director and staff working out of a central office on both commercial and community projects.

Commercial landscaping and contracting work is taken on at commercial rates by designers and architects, who estimate and manage work on behalf of public, commercial and private clients. Most contracts now require at least three tenders so the quotations have to be competitive for all clients – including the sponsors. The commercial groups also offer a consultative service to large groups such as the water authorities.

On the whole, community projects come from a number of different clients who own or have responsibility for derelict land. For example, a local community may request help from its council to clear and restore a fouled tip. If the council agrees, it will contact the Groundwork Trust office who in turn will offer a free consultative report and explain what grants are available. If the resources are available, and the contract is awarded, the Groundwork team will manage the project to completion and probably organize the maintenance for a period before handing it back to the local authority.

A typical project is the eight-acre 'Gypsy Site' at the intersection of three major roads south of St Albans. The area had been used by gypsies as a car scrapyard and by the locals (and others) as a general dump. The St Albans City and District Council decided to reclaim the area and approached the Groundwork Trust for an estimate and recommendations on the funding available. In the event, a plan costing £55,000 was agreed, 50 per cent to be funded by a Derelict Land Grant and the rest by the council.

Much of the money will be spent on the heavy contracting plant needed to clear the site, create the landscaping, smooth the contours and dig the ponds. However, some £15,000 will go on BTCV-type work – making the paths, planting trees, digging beds and completing the landscaping. When it is completed, the area will have been transformed from an eyesore into a pleasant place for such activities as walks and school nature studies.

Another St Albans conservancy project is the Water Cress Beds, originally a derelict area brought to the City Council's attention by the residents of the Riverside Road Conservation Group. A local project was set up including the Trust and representatives from the sponsors – the city council, Countryside Management Services, Wildlife Group and English Nature. The local conservation group has now taken responsibility for site maintenance.

ORGANIZING THE RELUCTANT

The second requirement of any work programme is organization. Most of the work carried out by BTCV and the Groundwork Trust is done by volunteers who are personally committed, keen to learn new skills and enjoy being with like-minded people. Although unemployed people work voluntarily with both groups, many team leaders have found it difficult to supervise people who are not there of their own free will. Voluntary organizations could almost certainly provide projects for the unemployed, almost enough for the likely numbers. But they would be reluctant to provide supervision for many people who would either prefer to do nothing or be somewhere else. Yet, one useful supervisory model could be the Community Service which organizes work for convicted offenders as a sentence of the court.

In 1974, the British government decided to introduce a form of community service as an alternative to custodial sentences handed down by magistrates' or crown courts. Sentenced offenders considered suitable for Community Service are seen by a Probation Service ancillary, the coordinator between the offenders and their clients. An ancillary will generally be someone who wishes to join the Service but needs to gain practical experience before starting professional training. They generally start in their mid-30s, by which time they will have done another job. Some very valuable people are rather older and are looking for a new challenge after a successful first career. They interview each individual, decide on their skills and assess the risk to potential clients if unsupervised work were allowed. Many work requests come from the social services on behalf of old people – perhaps to maintain their homes, dig gardens or help them with shopping. Other sources of work are voluntary organizations, like conservation groups or branches of local government.

Project supervision is organized by paid part-timers with leadership and, very often, trade skills. Their job is to supervise (sometimes truculent) young people on projects that may be quite boring and unfulfilling. Supervision is considered essential until individuals can be left to work on their own, usually after twenty-one hours of work. Supervisors have considerable powers of sanction. If offenders play truant, idle at work or deliberately perform badly they can be sent home and be required to serve the time again. The part-time supervisor's immediate superior is the Probation Service ancillary and, ultimately, the probation officer. Offenders can be returned to court for flagrant or continued abstention, or poor behaviour.

Any plan to use the Community Service to supervise the unemployed would be highly inappropriate, but such supervision could well employ its organizational principles. There are certainly projects within the community in abundance providing the work did not take jobs away from employed people.

. . . ENTER THE CEC

As Doctor Johnson observed: 'Depend upon it, Sir, when a man knows he is to be hanged in a fortnight, it concentrates his mind wonderfully.' So it is with rising unemployment. Money must be found to combat the wasting effect of joblessness and the accompanying threat of inner-city violence and increasing lawlessness. This proposal suggests a creative way forward.

Any work programme for the unemployed should consist of worthwhile projects, properly supervised and with an important element of training. To this might be added: payment should be related to the work and that those providing the work should be able to authorize payment in an effort to simplify the system. Many public and private organizations would provide work, in the same way that useful tasks were found for the CCC. Both BTCV and the Groundwork Trust have countless potential projects that would not normally be undertaken commercially. The trusts, both nationally and locally, have their own work programmes, which could well be expanded and run through their own central and local organizations. Their skills can be tapped to assess, categorize and cost each project, according to size, complexity, remoteness, required skills, necessary equipment and resources.

These and other voluntary organizations have ample skills to evaluate projects. BTCV in particular has the organization to manage 70,000 volunteers on a weekend basis. In the view of its chief executive, this could be expanded at least tenfold given time, through its own organization and that of its conservation training and managing associate, Conservation Practice Limited.

Based on the present work of BTCV, Groundwork and Community Service, each Civilian Environmental Corps (CEC) project might fall into one of three categories. **Level one** projects would be simple local undertakings involving supervised un-skilled individuals within a small radius of a central point. The work calls might come from several sources: the social services asking for assistance with old people's gardens, a village council needing help to paint the community hall or a town council wanting to clear litter. These would not be dissimilar from calls on Community Service.

Level two projects would involve skilled work undertaken by tradesmen or semi-skilled people capable of more specialized jobs. There may be some complications here because some of this kind of work might otherwise by taken by independent craftsmen or organizations working at a commercial rate. However, there should still be many public-work programmes that could not otherwise be afforded or undertaken – just like the CCC projects described earlier. Tradesmen would also play an essential training and supervisory role, not unlike the CCC's Local Experienced Men (LEM). Like the LEM they would be paid a premium for both their skill and their time as supervisors. Finally, **level three** projects would be on a larger scale and might require working away from home. The range would be considerable. BTCV have many projects in remote places such as Snowdonia or the High-lands of Scotland.

There may be a role for the armed services in organizing the remote camps. They have the capacity to run such structures, they have probably the finest training systems in the country, and, as the CCC found in the 1930s, the camps provided a wonderful environment for turning out leaders. The projects must be properly supervised. Every organization overseeing work projects has stressed the importance of planning, managing, executing, supervising, inspecting and signing-off a project.

It may be fortunate for the programme that some of the unemployed will have skills and leadership experience to organize and run projects at different levels. Potential leaders could be identified when they signed on for unemployment benefit. As suggested earlier, individuals should be offered the choice of support while working independently or operating within a government-sponsored programme. Those who chose the latter could then be further screened to single out the people immediately able to take charge of projects without any further training. For example a construction foreman might take charge of a level-two project and a supervisor a level-one project.

It is essential that the project leaders have sanctions, like Community Service supervisors, over individuals who may be reluctant participants. If, as is suggested, every project is properly quantified and costed, supervisors will only validate an individual's work sheet if a job has been completed to the standard and within the time set. Failure to do this would mean a rework until a satisfactory conclusion. Such a publicly funded programme could only work if supervisors were licensed by an appropriate authority, which would apply regulatory checks on individual performance.

TRAINING FOR A BETTER FUTURE

All the best work-creating programmes, like the CCC, Workfare in California and its Massachusetts equivalent have offered their participants training opportunities. Those working within the system should be given the hope that their time in unemployment would help them towards a better future.

Training could take place on various levels. As in California, welfare claimants should be given a basic writing, reading and maths test. If remedial work is needed, participants should be brought up to school-leaving standard. Then, the work itself will create different possibilities for technical training – in addition to basic field crafts such as tree planting, wall building and hedge laying there would be opportunities for training in anything from vehicle maintenance and surveying, to forestry and driving heavy equipment. Depending upon the project concerned, carpentry, metalwork, bricklaying, book keeping, catering could all be suitable subjects. This practical training could be a springboard leading to the attainment of one or other of the National Vocation Qualifications (NVQ).

Probably the most important training would consist of teaching people how to become successfully self-employed because, in all probability, a large minority of those in the working age group will not otherwise be able to find paid employment. Independent working will not attract everybody, and urgent thought should be given to making self-employment less risky than at present. True, enterprise courses and allowances may be satisfactory for those who have a clear vision and confidence in what they can achieve. Because of the web of existing state-support systems, unfortunately, most have not.

A FLEXIBLE FRIEND

Once the salary level had been set, any payment should be on the basis of work completed to specification. As explained earlier, all the BTCV and Groundwork projects have been properly specified and costed, making it quite possible to allocate work to individuals or groups and for them to be paid for results. There should be some system for remunerating 'waiting time' when a project is not available – probably paid at a lower rate.

If, as was suggested earlier, supervisors are given the authority to sign and authorize job sheets, there is little reason why payment should be made through the present bureaucratic system. Each claimant could be given a magnetic stripe 'credit card' programmed with personal details. This, plus a certified record of work done signed by the supervisor, could then be presented at an agency, such as the Post Office, which would effect payment – though clearly there would have to be safeguards and checks to prevent fraud.

EIGHT

KEEPING THE ROOF ON

Shortly before getting married in 1952, a husband-to-be received this advice from his prospective father-in-law: 'Never get involved with property, my boy. If you want a good investment, buy gilt-edged stock. You can't go wrong.' Wise words for the 1930s, no doubt, but hardly helpful after the war, when governments were hell-bent on a policy of inflation to maintain full employment. And inflation, of course, plays havoc with fixed-income stock. It only confirms the old Kondratieff maxim that wisdom skips a generation.

Forty years on, at least 50 per cent of the older man's advice appears more sound. As Christopher Fyldes, the economic commentator for the *Daily Telegraph*, points out, since World War II, the home has become an investment – like equity in a company, to be bought and sold for profit. Unfortunately, like stock and shares, house prices can go up as well as down and, for most people, losing a home is an infinitely greater misfortune than taking a loss when the stock-market tumbles.

What could be in store for the housing market in Britain? One answer is to consider what happened during the last low point of the Kondratieff cycle in the United States during the early 1930s. The American example is important because the level of speculation there in the 1920s was much greater than in Britain at the same time, when only one in five households was owner-occupied. During the 1980s, of course, housing speculation was rife on both sides of the Atlantic, which makes the comparisons with sixty years ago so interesting – and so significant.

AFTER THE FRENZY

One of the most important yardsticks for property prices is the house price/earnings ratio. This shows the kind of sums people are paying for houses, measured as a multiple of what they earn. To arrive at the ratio, the average price of a house, as reported by the *Journal of Housing Finance*, is divided by the average individual's annual earnings as published in the *New Earnings Survey*. Since 1956, the ratio has fluctuated between 3 and 3.5 – in other words, the average home owner has been paying between three and three-and-a-half times his or her annual pay for a house. As house prices were fuelled by demand in the housing speculation of 1973, the ratio rose to a high of 4.95 before returning to normal levels. In the last housing boom, it again rose above 4 in 1988, and remained there until 1991 when it peaked, once again at 4.95. By the first quarter of 1992 the ratio had sunk back to 3.55.

As a result of the house-buying frenzy, the number of mortgaged properties grew by over 50 per cent between 1980 and 1990. Over the same period house prices more than doubled. In 1983 the Halifax Building Society noted that the so called standard average house cost £30,898. In July 1989, at its highest point, it cost £70,588. For a time it seemed that the run would never end until, as the new decade began, the volume of new mortgage deals started to ebb and prices, particularly in the south-east of England, began to slip.

By October 1992, the Halifax standard average was 13 per cent off its peak, as £61,837 – and still falling. At that point, only those who bought after July 1988 would have been showing a loss. In August 1992, the Bank of England's *Quarterly Bulletin* reported that one in ten mortgaged home owners had negative equity averaging £6000. But if the slippage continues as it did in the comparable period of the early 1930s, and no government action is taken to arrest the slide, then by 1995 at least three million home owners will have negative equity – in plain English, their homes will be worth less than they paid for them. If, as seems likely, two-thirds of these are unable to keep up their interest and mortgage premiums, two million house owners could lose their properties and still remain in debt. The building societies and banks that lent them the money will face losses of over £30 billion, even after loans covered by mortgage-indemnity insurance have been paid.

The present British government has given every encouragement to home ownership, with tax relief for mortgage interest payments and inducements for purchasing previously rented homes, such as council housing. However, personal attitudes to home purchase could already be changing rapidly. After all, who wants to save up for a declining asset?

The number of people in private rented accommodation fell from nearly 20 per cent of households in 1970 to around 8 per cent in 1991. Council and housing-association rentals have also declined. The housing slump will almost certainly increase the demand for rented accommodation, in spite of tax incentives to buy. Indeed, more favourable tax treatment for landlords may be on its way. The 1988 Housing Act made a start by restricting tenants' rights. Now there is pressure on the government to equalize tax treatment of landlords so as to make renting more affordable for tenants. Possible areas for reform are capital gains tax, still levied on sales of rented accommodation (but not private homes), and VAT, payable on rents.

WHAT GOES UP

As discussed in chapter 2 housing obeys similar laws to other investments, running in rhythms like the Kondratieff long wave and the Kuznets US real-estate cycles. The US experienced its steepest fall in the 1890s and an even greater fall of 87 per cent in housing investment between 1927 and 1934. The collapse that began in 1927 followed rampant land speculation, particularly in Florida, when land plots changed hands rather like financial and commodity futures are traded at present. The bubble burst when the banks were forced to increase their interest rates and housing construction declined year by year until Democrat Franklin D. Roosevelt as newly elected president offered support to lenders who, by then, were repossessing houses at the rate of 1000 a day.

Roosevelt's mechanism was to introduce the Home Owners Loan Corporation (HOLC), a fund created from bank and public borrowings, which refinanced defaulting loans; eventually 20 per cent of the mortgaged market was underwritten to the undying gratitude of thousands of Americans. If they were not already Democrats, they would certainly have voted for the president at the next election.

By contrast, the Kondratieff trough of the late 1920s and early 1930s hardly affected British housing, probably because interest rates were unaffordably – for the time – high in the late 1920s, and so relatively few people owned their homes. In his book *The Downwave*, Robert Beckman reports that during the 1920s, the more expensive homes cost £2000, the smaller ones as little as

£600. A very highly paid workman (or a couple) earning £5 per week could save the down payment of £125 and raise a mortgage for 75 per cent of the purchase price repayable, with 5 per cent interest, over twenty years. By 1931, only one in five homes were owner-occupied, while the remaining families lived in rented accommodation.

The price of homes actually declined in the 1930s, and mortgage terms were relaxed so that a £500 house could be bought for a down payment of only 5 per cent (£25). This enabled those earning £4 a week to afford a down payment and the subsequent repayments plus interest. By 1939, the number of owner-occupiers had risen to one in four.

Housing investment in post-war Britain continued steadily although governments' stop/go policies meant that it went in fits and starts. At 1980 prices, housing investment grew from £3.5 bn in 1948 to nearly £9 bn in 1983 with huge associated increases in land and building prices. Beckman quotes from a 1972 paper by E.A. Vallis in the *Estates Gazette* that from 1948 to 1970 land prices rose eight times, from £10,000 per acre to £80,000. Building prices rose at a similar rate.

In 1980, according to the Council of Mortgage Lenders, there were 6.2 million mortgaged properties in Britain. By the first half of 1992 that had risen by nearly 60 per cent to 9.8 million, representing around 50 per cent of all households. Since the Council does not, in fact, represent all mortgage lenders, the real figure is almost certainly higher.

The traditional form of housing finance is the capital repayment mortgage, a loan which is gradually reduced by regular payments, usually over twenty-five years. The interest charge, allowable against tax for the first £30,000 of the loan, declines as the capital balance reduces. During the last housing boom, however, the repayment mortgage became less and less popular. By 1992, this type of mortgage comprised only 13 per cent of the total. Of the rest, 77 per cent were endowment mortgages.

With endowment mortgages, the borrower does not repay any capital. Interest on the full capital amount is paid monthly for the entire term of the loan. The borrower takes out an endowment policy (for a monthly premium), which matures at the same time as the debt must be repaid – again, usually after twenty-five years. By that time, it is hoped, the endowment will be worth at least the mortgage value, perhaps more.

Up to 1990, it was an ideal world for estate agents, lenders and borrowers; it was expected that the mortgage would run its natural course, the endowment mortgage would repay the loan, and the borrower would be left with a tidy profit. No longer. In 1992, house values are falling faster than loans, houses are being possessed from borrowers who lose their jobs and can no longer pay the monthly instalments, and lenders are being forced to suffer losses. Unfortunately this is all part of the Kondratieff downwave that every other generation seems destined to endure.

This condition of negative equity in which one's home is worth less than one paid for it could have serious impact on lenders as borrowers start to default in droves. They will then be – indeed already are – repossessing assets worth less than the original loan. By 1995, assuming a 60 per cent fall from the Halifax average price for 1990 of £68,900, total negative equity on homes bought between 1985 and 1992 will total £50 billion. If as suggested earlier, two-thirds of the affected borrowers default, the lenders will be the poorer by more than £30 billion.

DOWN BUT NOT OUT

How does the repossession process work and is there anything one can do about it? Technically, the process is quite simple. When repayments stop being made for any reason, the lender has the right to apply to the County Court, obtain a possession order and instruct the bailiffs to remove the householder and belongings. In practice it is rather more complicated: first, because the court, if approached wisely, may give a sympathetic hearing to a home owner facing eviction and, second, because lenders are realizing that selling repossessed houses becomes more difficult as more dwellings come on to the market.

The Council of Mortgage Lenders (CML) and SHAC, the London housing-aid centre, have published excellent guides for their members and clients which, if understood, will help those who are no longer able to make repayments and genuinely want to work out a solution with the lender. As far as the lenders are concerned many potential defaulting problems are caused at the moment of granting a loan. During the 1980s when many loans were being signed for three times salaries and for over 75 per cent of the price it seemed that the good times could go on for ever. During the depression, fewer things are certain. Many borrowers are made redundant and cannot pay; others who bought at the top of the market are reluctant to make repayments for an asset declining in value faster than repayments are diminishing their debt.

As soon as one or two payments are missed, a letter is sent to the borrower. The CML reports that in the vast majority of cases, the reason is an administrative oversight or a temporary income shortfall. If the account continues to be in arrears, several letters are sent, telephone or personal calls made to arrange a meeting with the borrower. Several lenders are now setting up helplines to open communications between the parties. Naturally, it is very much better for the borrower to admit and report a problem than wait to be tracked down.

Once a meeting has been arranged various remedies could be negotiated.

● The term of the repayment loan cann be lengthened, which could possibly help, but in many cases there is little significant difference to monthly repayments. An endowment mortgage can be surrendered and switched to repayments, but the policy may exact penalties for early cancellation.

● Part of the interest may be deferred, though this will not be a long-term remedy. It may be possible to capitalize interest – instead of paying it, add it to the amount already owed, ultimately resulting in larger repayments over the loan term. A mortgage rescue scheme could be negotiated, whereby an organization such as a housing association buys the property, taking it into their own stock, and the owner-occupier then becomes a tenant. This could be a useful arrangement if a transfer price could be easily negotiated – a matter of some difficulty with falling prices. The lender might advise the borrower to let the property or take in a lodger.

If none of the remedies proves successful, the lender will have little option but to sent a letter threatening to take legal proceedings. If the matter is still not resolved, details of the claim will be sent to a solicitor whose job is to apply to the county court for a possession order; in due course the borrower will receive a summons, a statement of the claim and a hearing date. Should the court judge the case to be hopeless then a possession order will be granted to the lender to take effect usually within twenty-eight days, though other periods may be awarded. If, by that time, the borrower has not remedied the position, the lender may apply to the court for a warrant of possession, under which the court bailiffs will evict the borrower.

This procedure gives no pleasure to the lenders. Not only will they be put to considerable trouble, they are also likely to show a significant book loss during a market downturn. The CML document outlines three ways a lender can take possession. One is by court order, providing all the legal procedures have been followed. Proceedings may be suspended should the court consider that the borrower can pay the outstanding sums in a reasonable time. The court may also delay an order to allow the owner-occupier to find other accommodation. After possession, the borrower is still liable for accrued interest and any price shortfall on sale, but lenders are seldom anxious to pursue the case through the bankruptcy courts.

A second route to repossession is by a borrower agreeing to sign a voluntary possession order when repayments are in arrears, and the property has failed to sell. However, the borrower is still responsible for any price shortfall and interest arrears, which can rise considerably if the house is slow to sell. Some indemnity insurers do cover voluntary surrenders, but if the loss on sale is small, the difference is usually written off.

The third alternative is that the house may be surrendered by the borrower leaving the dwelling and sending the keys to the lender. The solution has a certain simplicity, and the possessed house can be put rapidly on the market. As in all defaults, the borrower is still liable for accrued interest and any difference between the outstanding loan and the price received plus costs.

An indemnity insurance policy taken out in favour of a lender (paid for by the borrower) will often be required if the loan is greater than 75–80 per cent of the house price. In case of default, the lender will receive the difference between the purchase price and 75 per cent of the original price of the possessed house. Under the terms of the policy, the insurance company can pursue the borrower for the claim – by taking a charge on any new house purchases, for example.

THE HORSE MIGHT TALK

The story is told of a man, condemned to die, who begged for a year's stay of execution so that he could prove he had exceptional powers. In that time, he claimed, he could teach the king's horse to talk. If he was successful, he suggested, the quid quo pro should be a full pardon. Believing this impossible, the king agreed. When asked by the jailer what he thought he was up to, the man replied that in the course of a year anything could happen. The king might die, the man might die – or the horse might talk! For a borrower, a stay of execution could mean that money might be found, the lender might go bust or legislation might be enacted to delay repossession. Whatever the possibilities, there are several courses of action that, at worst, would delay proceedings and, at best, prepare the ground for a better deal.

If there is any possibility that the borrower could keep up partial repayments, they should approach a Citizens Advice Bureau (CAB) or debt advice agency to get help with preparing a statement and there are a number of charities that might help with payments. SHAC provides advice on mortgage payment problems. Borrowers should consult the *Directory of Grant Making Trusts* at the local public library or try other alternatives described in SHAC's *Rights Guide For Home Owners*.

The CAB has considerable experience in arguing a client's case with the court – particularly if the borrower has proposed a strict regime of cost savings. If the borrower has received a letter threatening legal action, they should write immediately to the lender informing them of measures to continue payments with the advice of the CAB or debt agency.

Once a summons has been issued, a borrower who believes he has a good case may request a hearing to be adjourned. However, this is often challenged by the lender arguing that it is up to the judge to decide an adjournment based on the evidence presented by both sides. Once a court hearing has been fixed, the borrower should arrange to be represented (with legal aid if necessary), particularly if the CAB or debt agency believe the case is sound. Even if a possession order has been granted, the court can still delay execution if new proposals can be made.

AVOIDING A HOUSING MELTDOWN

A housing meltdown on anything like the scale described would be savage. Of the possible three million homes with negative equity by 1995, most would seem at risk from a combination of financial crisis, massive unemployment and a deepening depression. Assuming that two-thirds – two million homes – would be at risk of repossession, this would represent 20 per cent of the mortgaged housing stock. This is the same percentage that Roosevelt's Home Owners Loan Corporation (HOLC) had to refinance in March 1933 when repossessions in the US were running at 1000 per day.

There is no reason for a house to be repossessed just because it has negative equity. Whether the owner is prepared to make repayments on a declining value is another matter; many borrowers would surely try to negotiate a deal whereby the lender and borrower agree to share a loss when the house is sold.

There have been several suggestions as to how the present housing crisis might be tackled. Late in 1991 when repossessions first caused a political furore, Chancellor of the Exchequer Norman Lamont announced that Stamp Duty on contracts of sale would be waived for a limited period. He also arranged for those on income support to get help with mortgage interest payments in certain circumstances, especially with first mortgages – though it should be noted that income support does not include endowment premiums. He also suggested that instead of exercising the right of possession, houses might be sold to housing associations, the previous owners then becoming tenants. In the Chancellor's

Autumn Statement he set aside £750 million to buy empty housing for low-rent occupation, saying that this would reduce the overhang by 20,000. However, in late 1992 there were an estimated 200,000 houses sitting empty at the moment, further depressing the market.

The borrowers-to-tenants plan has not been a success for various reasons, chief among them disagreements over the price at which the house would be transferred, who would bear the lender's costs, interest arrears and the like. And, anyway, most owners do not want to become tenants in their own houses. As a result, few have been transferred and the repossessions continue.

Another programme was proposed by Abbey National Building Society, which suggested that life could be injected into the housing market if government allowed those selling houses at below their original purchase price to recoup the difference as a tax allowance. Wisely, the government declined to commit the taxpayer to the huge potential downside risk this would entail.

If the housing market collapses on the scale envisaged earlier, injecting life into the housing market will be rather less important, and less feasible, than a plan to save both lenders and borrowers from ruin. Mindful of Franklin D. Roosevelt's HOLC scheme, any such plan would need at least four elements.

● A price floor to ensure there is a clearing level below which houses will be bought. The slippage in the housing market is unlikely to stop until such a floor is provided for house prices. A suitable level might be 60 per cent below the Halifax standard house price of £68,900 in 1990.

● A method to clear bad loans made by failed lenders. Many building societies will fail because of non-performing loans and low volume. IBCA, the European credit-rating agency, predicts that of the present ninety-plus societies, only thirty will survive the 1990s. The normal mechanism is for the strong to absorb the weak like the Woolwich absorbed Town & Country, but the bigger societies would also be put at risk by having to deal with a raft of non-performing loans.

● For those whose homes are likely to be repossessed, an alternative way to refinance their loans.

● Some form of government guarantee.

AN AMERICAN RESCUE PACKAGE

In 1933, Franklin D. Roosevelt introduced the Federal Deposit Insurance Corporation (FDIC), which insured depositors against bank failure. Each bank was required to pay an annual premium according to its size – the idea was that the accumulating premiums would be sufficient to bail out depositors. The role of the FDIC was to take over banks that had failed, write off non-performing loans, pay off the depositors and sell the remaining assets to another bank.

A similar programme was introduced for the US equivalent of building societies – the savings and loans (S&Ls) – called the Federal Savings and Loans Insurance Corporation (FSLIC). All went well until the early 1980s when many S&Ls became insolvent. It had been the American practice to lend at low fixed interest rates on the assumption that the federal government would maintain a stable currency. This touching faith in politicians was rewarded when many thrifts, as the S&Ls were called, found themselves having to pay depositors rates well in excess of 15 per cent during 1981, while many borrowers were paying 8 per cent or less.

The final irony of the S&L saga occurred in 1988 when the

government gave both the FDIC and the FSLIC federal guarantees. After many thrifts failed – often through wild speculation, malpractice and excess – the threat to the FSLIC was such that the central government was obliged to set up a special fund called the Resolution Trust Corporation (RTC). As with the banks, the RTC took on its books the non-performing loans, paid off its depositors and sold on the sound deals. The RTC was initially set up with a capital of $50 billion, but it is already costing the taxpayer many times this sum, and the US central government is now the largest private-property owner in the country.

ENTER THE NATIONAL HOME OWNERS RELIEF FUND

Borrowers in Britain most likely to have negative equity will be those who have acquired mortgages since 1985 or 1986. This is not to say that homes bought with 80 per cent loans negotiated before 1985 (in the case of endowment mortgages) and 1986 (repayment mortgages) will not be repossessed, merely that in those cases a loss to the lender will be less likely. The borrower, of course, will have lost all the staged payments but might finish up with some equity to spare.

Another American practice might provide a solution. There are several corporations, all under government guarantee, that buy clusters of mortgages. In effect, the S&L sells the mortgage and the income and rights that go with it, at a discount, to one of these institutions – the best-known are the Federal National Mortgage Association (Fannie Mae) and Federal Home Loan Mortgage Association (Freddie Mac). In a process known as securitizing, the mortgages are bundled together and sold on to investors in the form of participating bonds. The system adds liquidity to the housing market, because the S&L is now free to expand its lending.

Securitizing mortgage loans is not widely practised in Britain, but it could well be encouraged if the alternative was a collapse in housing finance. The system could work like this: the Building Societies Commission together with City institutions would establish a fund to act as a buyer of last resort for all mortgaged properties that would otherwise be repossessed. There would be much argument about the guaranteed price, but a value of 60 per cent below 1990 levels would probably not give the fund managers too much downside risk. They would be more cooperative if the Commission had secured the promise of a government guarantee. Let the fund be called the National Home Owners Relief Fund (NHORF).

If a borrower defaulted, the lender could offer its charge over the property to NHORF as a alternative to taking possession. Assuming a price could be agreed somewhere above the 60 per cent threshold, the charge would pass to the fund, and the borrower would be offered the chance to refinance mortgage payments at the house transfer price. The loan arrangements could continue to be managed by the original lender for an administrative fee.

If a bank or building society failed through non-performing loans or low volume, the fund would act as a buyer of last resort. The institution's bad loans would be sold to NHORF so that the bank or building society itself would be attractive to a buyer. NHORF could then securitize these mortgages, by issuing bonds in exchange for a number of loans – bonds that could then be subsequently traded. This solution would be similar to trading non-performing Third World debt at a considerable discount to its face value.

The arrangements would not please everyone. Clearly, the indemnity insurance companies would stand to suffer a considerable loss, since they would be obliged to pay out the difference between the original mortgage value and the price paid by

NHORF. On top of the £2 billion they had already lost by August 1992, they could reasonably expect to pay out a further £4.5 billion. Under the terms of the agreement, the insurance companies could seek to recoup at least some of the losses from the original borrower – even if this meant pursuing them to their next home.

Assuming a collapse of the magnitude suggested, lenders would have to write off some £30 billion after the indemnity insurances have been paid in. Writing off sums of this order – some 10 per cent of the £300 billion lent to the housing market – would bankrupt many of the small lenders, and the industry would be forced to contract. But the system would survive. Furthermore, the pain from many distressed borrowers would be considerably relieved, although the clear winners would be NHORF and the government's popularity.

As the housing market recovers, as it will in due course, the fund managers might decide to sell back some of the loans to the lenders; or they may choose to hold the mortgages to maturity. And, as Franklin D. Roosevelt discovered on his re-election in 1936, helping people keep their homes paid excellent electoral dividends.

NINE

A NEW MENU

The climate is changing, as we have observed. In 1993 and 1994, countries in North America, northern Europe and the CIS are likely to face cool and dry growing conditions, resulting in food shortages and rising prices. The shortages will not be limited to crops. They will extend to meat production – less animal feed means fewer animals. Even in developed countries, this chain of events will affect not only people's pockets but also their diets, and it may well encourage a return to growing one's own vegetables and keeping one's own livestock. In less developed countries the consequences may be more severe.

The way in which volcanic activity distorts normal weather patterns has already been discussed (see chapter 3). The most important influence on the weather at present is the aftermath of the June 1991 eruption of Mount Pinatubo in the Philippines, which discharged historically large amounts of dust and sulphur dioxide into the upper atmosphere. Over time, this volcanic effluence is cooling the weather and shifting rainfall from where it is needed to where it is not. The effects on world crop production will be compounded by the fact that, during the 1980s, the land area under cultivation declined by some 15 per cent. Many countries face the additional difficulties of deteriorating soil quality. During 1992, world carry-over stocks, which could in theory make up any shortfall, are at their lowest for twenty years.

GRAIN DRAIN

During 1993, the earth will suffer maximum cooling from a combination of volcanic detritus and much reduced radiation from sunspot activity. If history is to repeat itself, the price of wheat, soya beans and corn is likely to start rising sometime in 1993. Based on past eruptions, the following patterns could occur.

USA Corn (maize) production declined by 100 million tonnes in 1983 and 1988 and is quite likely to do the same in 1993. Taking the low carry-over stocks into account, this would create a large animal-feed shortfall – leaving little extra grain for exports.

CIS The former Soviet republics are likely to be the worst-hit, with the total grain harvest for 1993 being not much above 100 million tonnes. If the shortfall cannot be made up from imports, there is a strong chance of mass malnutrition and a mass movement of people westwards in search of food.

China The 'green revolution' of improving crop production that followed the return of land to China's peasants has seen a tremendous increase in output – in distinct contrast to the CIS. Although the northern wheat belt would suffer the same dry, cool climate as similar latitudes to Europe and North America, there is unlikely to be any substantial fall in output.

India The Indian rice crop constitutes nearly 60 per cent of the country's total grain production and is vulnerable to low-latitude volcanoes like Pinatubo. In 1987, the relatively mild Colombian volcano Nevado del Ruiz reduced yields by 20 per cent, so a much greater shortfall could be expected from Pinatubo, which was around 100 times more violent. A shortage of even 40 per cent (only twice that in 1987) would have a severe effect on a country with one of the world's lowest individual consumptions of grain.

Between them, eight grains or cereals provide 56 per cent of human energy and 50 per cent of the protein essential for cell structure. Between 1979 and 1981 wheat ranked highest in tonnage terms with 28 per cent of the total, corn came a close second with 27 per cent and rice third with 25 per cent. The balance was made up of barley (10 per cent), sorghum (4 per cent) and smaller amounts of oats, millet and rye. During the ten years to 1982, the output of wheat increased by 35 per cent, corn by nearly 49 per cent, rice by 28 per cent and barley by 27 per cent. Production of oats and rye declined by around 20 per cent.

Annual grain consumption varies considerably between rich and poor nations. In 1975, for example, each person in the United States consumed 708 kg, Soviet Union 540 kg, France 446 kg, China 218 kg, India 152 kg and Nigeria 92 kg. When the per capita annual consumption falls below 150 kg of cereal, the diet is generally supplemented by other crops, such as cassava and sweet potato.

Where the annual per capita consumption is above 200 kg, an increasing proportion of output is fed to animals. The US figure of 708 kg, for example, represents only 100 kg (or 15 per cent) consumed directly as bread, breakfast cereals and other obvious grain products. The balance was absorbed indirectly by eating animal and poultry products. Indeed, the developed world takes in most of its essential proteins through animal products.

CEREAL STORY

Cereals make very good use of arable land, yielding double the dry harvested weight per acre of most other crops, such as vegetable and oilseed. They are also very versatile and will grow in most latitudes, from rice in the tropics to rye in cool, dry northern latitudes. Cereals such as wheat and corn travel well with a high density. Oats and rice have a lower bulk density, and their husks or hulls have to be removed before they can be transported economically.

The United States remains the world's largest cereal producer, though China is catching up. Between 1979 and 1981, the US produced 19 per cent of the world's total cereals, followed by China with 18 per cent, the then Soviet Union 11 per cent, India 9 per cent and Canada 3 per cent. Europe's largest producer was France, with 1.5 per cent of the world total. The southern hemisphere grows relatively little, although Argentina and Australia rival French production with 1.5 per cent and 1.3 per cent of the total respectively.

WHEAT – FROM BROTHS TO BREAD

Wheat, rye and the hybrid triticale are the only crops containing gluten – an essential component for making bread. It was wheat that made the Industrial Revolution possible, because it was the cheapest and most efficient form of nourishment for labourers who had previously lived off the land on a diet of thin broth. When they moved into the new industrial towns, bread was a cheap, abundant, reliable and transportable food.

Wheat is thought to be the first crop to have been domesticated – between 18,000 and 12,000 years BC – and almost certainly formed the nutritional support of early Egyptian civilization.

With minimum preparation, seed could be sown and harvested by either stripping the grains or cutting off the spike containing the ears. The Egyptians discovered the unique baking properties of ground wheat, which subsequently developed into bread. Wheat can be grown at more northerly and southerly latitudes than almost any other crop, but it needs a good supply of rain. For every ton harvested it consumes 420 tons of water, a process called transpiration, which is partly a measure of the internal efficiency of the plant's metabolism.

The cereal is widely transported internationally because of its favourable bulk density, and it is one of the leading trading components of the CRB Index referred to in chapter 4. Wheat has also benefited from hybridization, whereby different strains have increased yield and made it adaptable to many climatic and growing conditions. Most wheat crops are planted in the autumn, as winter wheat, or later in the spring, and they have a growing season of around 100 days. They are, however, subject to 'winter kill' if unprotected by a protective barrier of snow. Snow also provides a trickle of moisture during the spring melt.

Wheat is grown in three basic forms. Hard red wheat grown in Canada and the United States is bread's main ingredient. When ground, it produces a strong flour, high in gluten, which causes leavening in the presence of yeast. Wheat is primarily consumed for energy although it also contains 11 to 14 per cent protein. About 72 per cent of the wheat kernel is used for flour, the balance being fed to livestock. There are numerous wheat strains used for bread flour; one is a hybrid with rye called triticale.

Soft wheat is grown primarily in western Europe and the wetter parts of North America. It has a lower protein content than the hard red variety, at between 8 and 11 per cent. Its soft quality and low gluten provides the essential quality for French bread with its wide texture and thick crust; however, it has to be baked throughout the day because it grows stale rapidly. Soft wheat is also used in biscuits, cakes, pretzels and breakfast foods.

Semolina is produced from a third wheat type called durum wheat. After soaking in water it is used in the manufacture of pasta, macaroni, spaghetti and noodles. These are often less nutritious than bread, as many of the nutrients are removed during milling. Durum wheat is high in protein and has been subject to considerable hybridization to find an acceptable colour. Wheat is also consumed as unleavened bread, without the addition of yeast, in flat bread or chapattis.

RYE – THE 'PIONEER' CROP

Rye can also leaven with yeast to produce rye bread. It is a particularly hardy grain, able to grow in poor soil and cool conditions – in some cases down to minus 35°C, which is much too cold for wheat. Its long root makes it tolerant and adaptable to widely variable conditions of soil moisture, erosion and acidity. It also has a shorter growing season than wheat and a higher protein content. Its hardy quality has earned it the label of 'pioneer' crop.

Rye is a diminishing crop in most areas but is increasing in the CIS, where efforts are being made to continue production in areas no longer suitable for wheat. The crop in also grown in Poland and Germany and some other areas like Argentina, South Africa and North America. Rye is not a good animal food; livestock find it indigestible, and the taste can be bitter if fed without blending.

Rye bread was most commonly eaten in northern and central Europe, but production slipped during the 1970s as people largely forsook the dark nutty texture for bread baked with wheat, and the area under cultivation declined by over 27 per cent. Other uses for rye are as a malt flavouring for whisky and in products like pumpernickel.

TRITICALE – BEST OF BOTH WORLDS

This is a manmade hybrid of wheat and rye (the Latin word for wheat is *triticum* and for rye, *secale*). The ear resembles wheat more than rye, but it has fibres or hairs like barley. When developed fully, triticale is likely to be a quality food for people and livestock, with a protein content of between 11 and 22 per cent, higher than both its parents. It supplements wheat, barley, corn or sorghum as an energy source.

Triticales's growing season is two weeks longer than wheat, which means that the correct planting time in the autumn must be chosen to avoid frost damage. The cereal has poor tolerance at present when not grown under correct conditions; however, it has a potential for growing in acidic, dry, or extreme conditions not suitable for wheat.

Triticale is milled and prepared in procedures similar to wheat but yields around one-sixth less of the dry weight. Some of the protein advantage is lost when milled into white-bread flour. The flavour of the finished product is equivalent to mild rye bread, and, when blended with wheat flour, triticale produces a meal with a high protein and amino-acid content. It is also good for pancakes, waffles, biscuits and cakes, but the flour is considered too dark for tortillas and chapattis.

CORN – STARCH, SYRUP AND SILAGE

Corn or maize was cultivated by the Native Americans of North America, Mexico and Central America long before Europeans settled there. It could be planted with the minimum of soil preparation in forest clearings and on hills. The newcomers leaned how to plant the crop in narrow rows with little or no cultivation in between, and now its production is highly mechanized with starter fertilizer, tillage, seeding and pesticides control all accomplished in a single action or pass.

Corn has become the major crop in the United States because its particularly efficient metabolism results in more than double the yield of wheat for the same planted area. It also uses water more efficiently, with a transpiration ratio of 350 tons of water per ton harvested, considerably less than wheat, rice, barley, oats and rye. Corn is also highly adaptable, and its hybrids will grow in a wide range of latitudes and altitudes. Many variations are grown, such as flint corn, popcorn and sweet corn.

Its disadvantage is that it is particularly vulnerable to below-average conditions. Corn cannot tolerate freezing temperatures, which makes it particularly susceptible to early frost damage before harvesting. It is also highly susceptible to dry conditions in July, which can shrivel the 'silks' that grow out of the cobs, so reducing germination and yield. A further limitation is that it can not be planted or harvested in bulk when the ground is too wet for machinery.

Corn has provided a staple diet in countries where is grown naturally, such as Mexico, where 98 per cent of the crop is consumed as tortillas, a type of flat unleavened bread. It is also used extensively to feed animals. In North America, 85 to 90 per cent of the crop is consumed on farms, where it is fed to livestock either as forage or silage.

Corn has a wide variety of food, drink and industrial uses. The immature leaves and fully grown cobs with soft milky kernels can be eaten as vegetables. Dry mature kernels can be ground into meal, flaked or shredded for breakfast food. Corn oil is extracted to be used as a salad or frying oil and popcorn is a popular snack. Food additives are produced by wet milling followed by separating starch and protein in a centrifuge. Starch is then converted into corn syrup, used in place of sugar in the food and beverage industry. The starch products are also widely used in non-food applications, such as gypsum, hardboard, adhesives and paper coatings. Corn is also used to produce methanol, alcohol, organic acids, vitamins and bourbon whisky.

RICE – FEEDING A THIRD OF THE WORLD

One-third of the world's population relies on ten ounces of rice per day for 80 per cent of its calorie intake and much of its protein. Rice production has risen prodigiously through the use of hybrids, fertilizers and improved cultivation. In the twenty years from 1960 to 1980, world output rose 108 per cent while the area under cultivation increased by only 8 per cent.

Like wheat, rice produces the best yields in dry-land conditions, in a temperate climate. However, by far the largest crop is grown in the submerged soil culture of the Asian lowlands, where the land is poorly drained. Paddy rice, the only major crop that can be grown in standing water, has a system of tubes that transport oxygen from the exposed leaves to where it is needed at the roots – something not possible with other cereals. There is also a deep-water rice, which takes root in the soil while the stem floats on the water. Rice consumes more water per ton harvested than any other cereal, with a transpiration ratio of 628. The peak yields are to be found in temperate areas between 49 degrees north and 36 degrees south although some hybrids cannot tolerate temperature above 22°C. Hybridization has developed some strains that mature in 100 days, allowing three or more crops per year.

The size of rice farms varies tremendously from 5000 acres in developed countries, such as the United States, to 2.5 acres and below in South-East Asia. Some Californian farms are highly mechanized. Their fields are levelled by laser beam, they are sown from the air, and the harvesters are designed not to bog down in the wet conditions.

The nutritional value of rice is highest when it is unmilled or brown rice. Rice milling removes the husk to leave part of the kernel intact. Further milling reduces the kernel to produce white or polished rice with a lower nutritional value. The proportion of proteins, fats and vitamins decreases with milling and the percentage of carbohydrates increases. Threshed or paddy rice is normally prepared by soaking the ears in water then parboiling to gelatinize the starch. The process increases the nutritional value by infusing proteins and vitamins from the outer portion and making it less prone to insect penetration when stored. The kernels are then slowly dried and the outer layer removed.

Brown rice takes nearly twice as long to cook as white rice. Polished rice loses much of its goodness but can be cooked more quickly. However, there is a half-way stage of light polish when the ear becomes pale golden, the taste excellent, and it loses only 1 per cent of weight compared to polishing. Apart from boiling, rice can be used in soups, puddings, as an addition to the brewing process and as a food filler. It is also made into a beverage (Japanese sake), into breakfast and baby foods, and it provides a source of industrial starch.

OATS AND BARLEY – DECLINING POPULARITY

Oats have historically been used for feeding livestock and horses because they contain the highest quality and quantity of protein. But both oats and barley have lower yields than wheat, and both have declined in importance in the last 200 years. In the decade to 1981 oat production declined by nearly 20 per cent worldwide, except in the USSR, where it rose by one-third. In the same period, demand for malt increased barley production by 20 per cent.

Neither crop has found favour as a food. Once the sacred crop of the ancient Greeks, barley is today primarily used as a source of malt for brewing. Oat flour, after rolling and milling, makes oatmeal cakes and porridge with high energy and protein value.

Oat grains, with their high hull content, can not be transported economically.

Oats and barley can grow in conditions of low fertility, exhausted soils and cool conditions down to -8°C, in areas not suitable for wheat. They are also tolerant to late sowing and poor cultivation and are resistant to diseases and insects, which makes them good organic crops. On the downside, both crops need considerable quantities of water and have poor resistance to lodging (the stems bend over and break). Although both have a growing season of eighty days, they are not suitable for winter seeding, and oats in particular does not readily produce adaptive hybrids to increase yield.

GREEDY MEAT

Cereals are an indirect as well as a direct source of human sustenance. They form an important part of the diet of livestock. Many animals can only exist if their grazing diet is supplemented by feedstuffs in the winter – mainly corn and soya beans. Meat production absorbs over 80 per cent of US corn production and receives the lion's share of government farming support in many countries. In 1990, for example, livestock farmers in the industrialized nations that comprise the Organization for Economic Cooperation and Development (OECD) received two-thirds of a total $123 billion in farming subsidies. This consumption is not confined to OECD countries. In the CIS, meat consumption has tripled since 1950, and feed consumption quadrupled; livestock now eat three times as much grain as people, and animal feedstuff imports have soared.

Such is the demand for meat that many Third World farmers now earn more by growing animal feed than by growing food for humans. It has been estimated that, if US per capita meat consumption were equalled by the rest of the world's population, total world grain output would need to grow by 250 per cent.

Meat production is not a very efficient use of food resources, however, because animals are not very efficient at converting what they eat into what, from a human perspective, is the final food produce. Pound for pound, cattle convert only 20 per cent of their nutritional intake into meat at the end of the day. None the less, the scale of the demand for animal feeding is considerable. By the early 1990s, there were globally three domestic animals to every human. By far the largest species are fowls (11 billion) followed by cattle, pigs, sheep and goats (around 4 billion in all), and the numbers have doubled since mid-century. In some cases, the numbers go with size of population, for example, China has 350 million pigs, 40 per cent of the world total.

The animals provide more than food, though. In Asia and Africa, nearly 90 per cent of the land is ploughed by draft animals, and the manure is a precious fertilizer and fuel. The rich countries prefer to eat their livestock. They produce 60 per cent of the world's meat, over 50 per cent of the eggs and nearly three-quarters of all milk, and consumption reflects this. In 1990 Americans ate 112 kg of meat per person, compared with 71 kg in Britain and 2 kg in India.

LOSING ENERGY

Large areas of cropland now produce grain for animals. Roughly 38 per cent of the world's grain (particularly corn, barley, sorghum and oats) is fed to livestock. The pattern varies considerably. In the United States, some 70–80 per cent of all domestic grain consumption is fed to animals; in India and in the sub-Saharan Sahel, the figure is only 2 per cent. Fish-meal used to be added to feed grains to complement the calorie intake, but it has gradually been replaced by protein-rich soya beans. In times of food shortage, however, the efficiency with which animals convert grain into energy deserves closer attention.

Cattle Cattle are ruminants that consume three-quarters of their nutritional intake from grass, hay and other fodder. However, since they are poor converters, the remaining one-quarter demands around one-third of all animal feed grain – some 4.8 kg of grain for every kilogram of meat. As half the grain and hay fed to US beef cattle is grown on irrigated land, it is estimated that 3000 litres of water are needed to produce one kilogram of beef.

Pigs Pigs are not grazers but are content with kitchen scraps and a grain-based diet. Pork is the most expensive meat to produce, needing 6.9 kg of feed for every kilogram of meat produced.

Poultry Poultry and pigs between them consume some two-thirds of all animal feed grains. In the case of poultry, national production efficiencies vary. In the United States, for example, it requires only 2.8 kg of feed to produce one kilogram of poultry meat, about half the feed needed by CIS farmers. Even so, poultry convert some 40 per cent more efficiently than beef and 60 per cent more than pigs.

Goats Goats and sheep are critical to the survival of poorer people. In the Sahel, for example, goats and sheep provide nearly 30 per cent of the meat, 16 per cent of milk and are essential providers of fibre, hides and manure. They also have value as barter and provide a living for between 30 million and 40 million herdsmen around the world. However, goat grazing damages the topsoil; with overgrazing, weeds with less of a root anchorage take the place of grass, and the topsoil becomes eroded by rain and wind.

DISH OF THE DAY

The climate changes discussed earlier in chapter 3 could mean a grain shortfall of 200 million tons in 1993–4 in the US and CIS. Unfortunately, any grain loss is unlikely to be made up from reserves, which have been the lowest for two decades. Cooler, drier weather will mainly affect animal feedstuffs, such as corn and soya beans, and the primary sufferers will be the poor feed converters, such as pork and beef. The feedstock shortfall could reduce the availability of pork (except in China, with its abundance of pigs) and beef by around one-third. The position will be made worse if the depression forces governments to reduce subsidies for animal production. When the New Zealand government recently eliminated subsidies to agriculture, the use of pasture herbicides and fertilizers fell rapidly, and the sheep herds were reduced from 70 million to 58 million (a reduction of 17 per cent).

In one sense, a reduction of meat consumption could be in line with existing trends. In the United States, for example, red-meat consumption has declined by 14 per cent since 1976. In Britain, six million people eat meatless meals most of the time. None the less, a meat shortage in western nations would change many diets in a way not seen since World War II and its aftermath, before food rationing came to an end. Since then, the food industry has provided the majority of people in the west with a tremendous range of nourishments, with great efficiency. The states of eastern Europe have been less fortunate; there a combination of uncertain weather, inefficient farming and poor distribution have precipitated a crisis that can only become worse as the 1990s progress.

WAR FOOD

During World War II, ironically enough, food shortages meant that most Britons ate more healthily than they do now. At the start of the war there were two gifted men at the head of the Food

Ministry: Sir Jack Drummond and Lord Woolton. Sir Jack Drummond was by training a nutritional biochemist whose work on butter and margarine substitutes had earned him a professorial chair at the age of 31; he was co-author of *The Englishman's Food*. a pioneer study of British diet since the Middle Ages.

From 1939, Drummond was chief scientific adviser at the Ministry of Food, where he applied his knowledge to the subject of diet in wartime. The minister for Food was Lord Woolton; as Sir Fred Marquis, Woolton had been the managing director of Lewis's, the Liverpool department stores. The two became a formidable team – Drummond the expert, Woolton the politician and communicator. They established a diet that was both nutritious and – through rationing – available to everybody. Butter and sugar were rationed goods that were in constant supply. Bread and potatoes were not rationed, but there was a supplementary points system providing an element of choice for 'luxuries' such as sultanas, sardines and condensed milk.

Both the scale and pattern of consumption has changed since then, as an increasingly health-conscious population eats more vegetables and fruit and a declining amount of meat and fish, as the table shows.

AVERAGE ADULT FOOD CONSUMPTION PER WEEK IN OUNCES

	PRE-WAR	WARTIME	1950	1981	1989
Fresh meat	28*	17	14	23	19
Bacon and ham	6	4	5	5	5
Fish	n a	n a	7	5	5

*This figure is questionable compared to post-war although those who could afford it ate meat at meals three times a day.

	PRE-WAR	WARTIME	1950	1981	1989
Potatoes	n a	n a	62	39	36
Other vegetables	n a	n a	34	40	46
Fruit	n a	n a	18	23	32
Sugar	16	8	10	11	8
Cheese	12**	3	3	4	4
Milk (pints)	n a	n a	5	4	3
Confectionery	6	3	n a	n a	n a

**Including milk solids but excluding butter.

HEALTH IN HARD TIMES

If meat consumption were to continue to decline, it would only confirm the present trends towards more healthy living. Already, the World Health Organization (WHO) has recommended that the calorie intake from fats be no more than 30 per cent, compared with the existing 37 per cent for most advanced nations at present. Nutritionalists recommend lowering the content still further to reduce most diseases of affluence. The US Surgeon General reported that, in 1987, 68 per cent of all deaths were caused by diseases of dietary excess and imbalance – problems that now rank among the leading causes of illness and death in the United States.

While health consciousness provides a motive of choice, there may be more compulsory reasons for a change in diet, as income and availability is squeezed simultaneously. Overall, this would steer households away from more expensive pre-packed food towards fresh products. The process would be accelerated if governments were forced to make some pay for health services (see chapter 6), which might encourage people to take more preventative care of their health through diet.

In the cooler drier times forecast earlier, the solution for many will largely depend upon what is available. If red meat (as the produce of high consumption of scarce grains) is much more expensive then many will turn to chicken or, possibly fish, if their farming can be shown to be more economical. If wheat yields are low then more attention will turn to rye, barley or oats – in fact, rye and triticale may become much more prominent foodstuffs in the 1990s.

Other foods may also become more popular. Buckwheat, a staple in Russia and Poland for a millennium, is used in Britain and France as a pancake base and will be a useful additional resource if other foods become scarce. Millet is a grain high in protein, low in starch and rich in minerals, and it can be combined with buckwheat in a dish served either hot or cold with a green salad. Bulgar or cracked wheat is eaten in the Middle East, where it is cooked to make a cake and then eaten with fresh vegetables. Island communities and the Japanese eat seaweed, which is rich in minerals and is highly nutritious. The Japanese variety is called *arame* and can be bought in some of the larger supermarkets and food stores.

If vegetables become expensive, then many will be encouraged to grow their own. Many gardens could be put to use growing vegetables in place of flowers or even lawns that could become unsightly with less rain and a ban on sprinklers. In towns, where home owners have less space, it is quite possible that disused factories, halls or warehouses could be converted to hydroponic growing of vegetables. This involves covered systems in controlled atmospheric conditions where correctly balanced nutrients are mixed with water before being piped to the plants.

If meat does become more expensive, expect dishes made from the following to become popular; leeks, onions, brussel sprouts, broccoli, cabbages, cauliflowers, carrots, marrows, courgettes, spinach, parsnips, turnips and potatoes. If the weather does not become too rough then peas, beans, lettuces and tomatoes can be added to the list.

This environment will bring opportunities, as always, for those entrepreneurs quick enough to recognize them and energetic enough to do something about the change in world menus. Opportunities for designing and preparing alternative foods – eat-in or take-away – will be many and various. Small bakeries could grow by offering a wide range of grain-based foods. Health and fitness training services should be much in demand – just as these were in the 1930s – and there should be opportunities for designing and tending the new gardens of the 1990s.

TEN

LIFEBELTS FOR BUSINESS

anaging a business during this 1990s depression will be quite different from getting through the recessions of the 1970s and early 1980s. Then, it was a matter of trimming costs, selling surplus assets and waiting for the storm to blow over. Now, hiving off non-critical operations will be just the start. Managing during debt deflation requires a different emphasis from normal business-cycle operations. Balance-sheet security becomes more important than maximizing profitability, operating in lucrative niche markets a sounder principle than keeping market share. Of greatest importance will be the need to maintain the rates of innovation and development during a time of static or declining prices.

One of the reasons that the game has changed so radically is that the bad times are going to last considerably longer than in past recessions. Another is that asset values will decline faster than debt, making it much harder to reduce the burden of loans. Probably the most difficult thing to deal with will be a likely fall of one-third in sales volumes from 1990 levels, spread over several years. These harsh conditions will force managers to lower their fixed costs considerably; they will become adept at subcontracting many of those activities it used to seem essential to keep within the business.

The process is only just starting. It is highly probable that human ingenuity will provide managers with a wide range of options – only some of the most vital will be described here. It is amazing what can be achieved when change is inevitable. This chapter describes the usual business-cycle crisis management that has been appropriate for most recessions since World War II, followed by the new techniques that will become a feature of managing a business in a depression. It discusses 'third generation' methods of cost reduction and 'shamrock' organizations that convert fixed to variable costs, allowing companies to lower their break-even points; it also gives some examples.

MISMANAGEMENT NEVER CHANGES

Learning how to manage the business cycles described in chapter 2 should be just as important as training in marketing, finance or information technology. These cycles have occurred regularly for at least 200 years, yet there is no reason to believe that anyone – be they politician, economist, banker or business person – has learned anything from the past. Perhaps the hope that 'this time it will be different' explains why people make the same mistakes each time, every cycle.

In *The Independent Director*, it is argued that every board should have at least one contrary thinker, someone who questions the current mood of optimism or pessimism, encouraging or cautioning as appropriate. These people are not universally popular – particularly when the rest of the board is committed to headstrong action or excessive pessimism – but they are essential, nevertheless.

Ideally, companies should always have such strong balance sheets and flexible management systems that they can ride any economic storm, and, of course, some of the largest do have this stability. Other businesses lack the financial and market firepower needed to duck and weave, riding out one storm and then climbing the wave of opportunity for the next cycle. It is as if different commanders were needed for each phase; a defensive manager for bad times and an offensive performer for booms.

As Joseph Schumpeter, the economist, observed in *Business Cycles*: 'It is easy to make profits when demand exceeds supply. It requires brains to manage in a recession.' Noted insolvency practitioner Michael Jordan, senior partner and chairman of accountants Cork Gully, believes that the root cause of every corporate descent into receivership is mismanagement.

The excessive booms of the 1920s and 1980s were fuelled by managers who borrowed great sums of money to expand their businesses, in many cases paying extravagant sums for acquisitions. Now, in the 1990s, they are caught in the debt trap, a common phenomenon after a boom. Having raised debt for acquisitions in a euphoric market, they have discovered too much was paid for a company unlikely to meet its profit targets.

Those who advised and funded these companies also got it spectacularly wrong – though, miraculously, they seemed to keep their jobs. Mismanagement can take different forms. Another noted insolvency specialist, Bill Mackie, identified several tell-tale signs that a company might be about to run into trouble.

● The company had recently erected a prestigious office building with a fishpond inside and a flagpole outside.

● The chairman was noted for his personalized number-plate, the smartness of his motor car and for public works outside the business.

● The company had recently won the Queen's Award for Industry.

● The chairman had a thriving after hours relationship with his secretary.

Although some symptoms of mismanagement can only be observed by those close to the company, ominous signs may occasionally be detected in the hieroglyphs of the chairman's statement. During the last recession, in August 1980, the *Financial Times*'s Lex Column reproduced some examples of the double-speak, complete with translation.

● 'The company reports that it is well placed to take maximum advantage of any early improvement in business conditions.' We are keeping our fingers crossed and hoping that things will get better.

● 'I am happy to say that we now have the facilities available to allow a substantial increase in our level of production.' We are on a three-day week.

● 'The directors know of no reason for the sudden fall in the ompany's share price.' The directors know of a very good reason for the sudden fall in the company's share price.

● 'The dividend has been adjusted to a level from which a progressive policy can be resumed in the future.' The dividend has been cut.

· RECOVERY MANAGEMENT ·
THE OLD WAY

It is a commonplace that those who have made a mess of running a company are seldom those capable of putting it right. Company 'doctors' called in to save a business or receivers trying to realize assets have nearly always encountered the most sublime optimism on the part of the incumbent executive directors. Perhaps the human spirit should be perpetually optimistic, but more is at stake than personal vanity. A failure often means creditors being defrauded, jobs lost, productive assets broken up and shareholders wiped out.

Saving a business in normal times is normally handled in two stages: first, stop the haemorrhage; second, return the business to profitability. Companies ultimately fail because they run out of money. This generally happens after losses have destroyed the balance sheet, and every bit of available credit has been exhausted. Anyone coming in as a white knight to rescue a company should be aware of the pitfalls because there are now considerable penalties for mismanagement and defrauding creditors.

This does not aim to be a turnaround handbook. And while taking the right action is one thing, convincing secured creditors (mostly banks) that they should support a rescue attempt and not call in the receivers is quite another. However, the following important steps should be taken.

● Appoint an individual to take charge of the rescue attempt. He should immediately prepare a recovery package, endorsed by the board, for approval by the secured creditors.

● Appoint a hard money man as the main cheque signatory.

● Cut all revenue and capital expenditure items to the bone.

● Stop all inessential cheques above a certain level – unless authorized by the main signatory.

● Stop all recruitment, curtail all new liabilities, such as advertising campaigns, and cut down drastically on expenses – particularly foreign travel.

● Collect all overdue debts that have been held up, often with trifling excuses such as a missing credit note. Some debtors are notorious for holding up payment if they think a company is about to fail.

● Sell excess assets and stock that can be turned rapidly into cash.

Sometimes, even in boom times, these measures do not work, in which case creditors should be informed immediately. Penalties for directors who allow a company to trade while insolvent are now too severe to go on hoping for a light at the end of the tunnel.

The return to profit is classically described as a reduction of costs while funding debt from asset disposals. This requires a staged programme of analysis and action to build up a business anew around the most profitable assets. The rescued company is likely to be quite a different shape after a successful rescue package, which would be illustrated by a comparison of the before and after accounts.

Consolidated sales should be lower once unprofitable companies or produce lines have been sold or shut down, and margins will be higher, thanks to reduced direct and indirect costs. Borrowings will be lower, paid down from asset disposals. Productivity will be increased, with the fewer remaining staff concentrated on the most profitable work. Assets will be written down to realistic values, and almost invariably the new worth of the company will be reduced. Finally, the break-even point will be considerably lower, allowing the business to trade profitably at a lower volume than before.

This plan works, most of the time, because profit margins can be raised through some price increases, and debt can be repaid with assets sold at reasonably close to balance-sheet values. Things are different during a debt deflation because asset values decline faster than debts, and competitive constraints do not allow for price increases. Both factors force managers to accept a new set of rules.

NEW RULES – SHRINKING TO GROW

Just how difficult it may be to keep a company profitable during debt deflation can be judged from the decline of volume and prices endured by American business during the 1930s. Between 1929 and 1933 manufacturing volume dropped by 40 per cent. Car production at General Motors declined by 70 per cent, primarily in the more expensive end of the market. Remarkably, the company never passed its dividend. But few conventionally structured businesses could remain solvent under such an onslaught, which is why managers will need to learn new working methods, command structures and forms of asset distribution.

One of these is 'downsizing', which squeezes out costs by reducing the scale of operations. IBM and British Telecom are already looking at reducing accommodation costs by siting employees at home and linking them to the central computer. Although these ideas might be sufficient in a business-cycle recession, they are unlikely to reduce break-even points to the necessary one-third of 1990 sales levels.

There are two well-tried management techniques that could do the job, however. They are complementary and could both be used by the same organization. The first is the 'third generation' approach, a term first coined in *Avoiding Adversity*. It operates at the leading edge of a company by converting the fixed costs of selling, service and distribution into a variable operating expense. The second is what Charles Handy, visiting professor at the London Business School, describes as the 'shamrock' organization. This technique operates at the input end of the business, working on a similar principle of transforming fixed production costs into the variable costs of subcontracting. Both techniques are destined to become widely understood and adopted in the 1990s.

A THIRD-GENERATION FACE TO THE CUSTOMER

A company with a large full-time sales or service force, for example, might decide that the team could do just as good a job working independently on a commission-only basis. The sales force could buy its independence, allowing the parent to operate at a much lower fixed cost. Variable costs would be increased, as the company would now have to pay full agency commissions, not merely bonuses to employees, and the profit margin would assume a flatter curve as a result. But the company's chances of surviving the depression would be greatly improved, because its break-even point would be firmly lower.

Conventionally minded managers may be shocked at the thought of releasing control of retail or wholesale outlets, but the principle has been well proven by the growth of franchising and the use of sales agencies. Companies taking the decision to put their shops or depots on to a third-generation footing not only reduce their own costs but almost invariably find that people working for themselves (within a disciplined operating system) outperform employees doing the same job. There are three different possible options – franchising, remote working and agency working.

FRANCHISING – MORE THAN FAST FOODS

Franchising is a fast-growing technique for expanding retail, distribution and service operations by replicating existing and successful, internal operations outside the company. The head office is relieved of many costly administrative functions and at least one tier of management can be removed. The technique can also be used for reducing the fixed cost of existing branches, depots or groups of people, such as a sales or service force. The singular advantage of franchising is that independent individuals or companies buy the outlying assets or facilities and operate these under licence from the parent. The new owners are then responsible for all aspects of their own administration, accounting, sales and operations.

Alert managements are already using franchising as a means of positioning themselves in the market-place. Consider the example of Dollond & Aitchison (D&A), Britain's leading ophthalmic dispensing group, which carries out eye tests and provides prescription lenses, frames, sunglasses and associated material. As a matter of policy, the company decided to concentrate activity in major town centres and embarked on a programme to franchise those practices that lay outside these areas.

Converting an outlet to a franchise is a relatively easy transition for the present managers; they know the routines, the customers and the products, which makes it much more simple to raise the necessary conversion finance. The major change is in attitude. Ownership concentrates the mind, and it is common for a franchise to increase sales by at least 20 per cent compared to a managed outlet. In the case of a D&A conversion, the new unit trades under the same name, buys frames and lenses from the franchiser at special rates but is financially independent. D&A receives cash for the assets transferred and a royalty of 7.5 per cent on sales.

Franchise opportunities are not restricted to the distributive trades. Company X supplies a technical and inspection service to a wide variety of companies, including oil refineries and process plants. It operated through several branches, which were all administered from head office in the north-east of England. It was making a marginal profit of less than 1 per cent on sales. Following a study by an outside firm of consultants, the branches have been franchised as separate limited companies, including all their previous assets and appropriate working capital. The companies were sold to the branch managements at written-down asset values. If they were reluctant to buy, the operations were offered to suitably qualified purchasers. Any transfer of ownership included pension-fund rights, and redundancy was paid to those losing their statutory rights.

The transfer of administration, branch management and accounting to franchisees reduced layers of head-office management. The central-office team now includes technical, franchise, marketing and general management people with the minimum of accounting, personnel and other staff. The sale of assets to the franchisees has radically strengthened company X's balance sheet, and it is now significantly more profitable. Franchisee sales would have to drop over 50 per cent before the company fell below break-even point. At the same time, income per employee has increased more than 300 per cent.

Successful franchising needs careful planning, as well as franchisees with a strong will to succeed. The franchisee, who will pay a fee for being set up and trained, needs an adequate margin and assurance of support and supply. An initial franchise feasibility report, evaluating the opportunities for both parties, should be followed by the formulation of a franchise plan, complete with manual, prospectus, agreement and promotional material. Then the format should be tested over twelve months in, say, three areas where franchisees are to be sought.

REMOTE WORKING

In the early 1980s photocopier manufacturer Rank Xerox embarked on a drastic reconstruction and now provides an excellent example of remote working in practice. The company realized it needed to adjust to the fierce competition it anticipated when the original Xerox patents expired – as they were soon to do. One particularly imaginative programme converted up to sixty professionals from full-time employees to the new status of independent businesspeople selling their expertise for a fee to their original employer. The company benefited by converting the fixed cost of employment to the variable cost of fees; the individuals scored by being set up in business with at least part of their income secured.

The first trial along these lines was conducted by personnel manager Roger Walker who agreed to be the guinea pig. Walker set up Chamberlains Personnel Services at Stony Stratford near Milton Keynes. It was agreed that he should be paid statutory redundancy and one year's salary for providing the parent with part-time recruitment and training services. Walker was also free to ply for other business apart from Rank Xerox's. The company did not leave him in the cold – it appointed a core manager as his regular contact and installed a computer terminal in his office for continuous communication with head office.

The programme was a success. After one year Walker reported on progress, and Rank Xerox decided that others should follow – over time, sixty more. The company saved about two-thirds of the previous employment costs of the individuals concerned and found the arrangement considerably increased internal efficiency, particularly in the way people spent their time – a 100 per cent improvement was typical. The company learned to manage subcontractors, not employees. It changed many attitudes, particularly of those who formulated, put out to tender and monitored contracts.

The stages in creating a remote-working regime are similar to those in franchising, with the notable difference being that each plan should be tailor-made in terms of an individual's particular skills and future relationship with the parent. Again, the plan needs to benefit both parties. The remote worker should be assured of a guaranteed income for the first year and, if assets such as a car and other kit are involved, these should be transferred at reasonable prices.

A member of staff from the parent company should be detailed to provide training and counselling services before and after the conversions to remote working. Once the programme has been agreed, it needs to be tested with one or more people or groups to prove that it works successfully. The initial programme needs to be monitored very carefully to ensure that both parties grow into the new relationship: the parent must learn to specify, put out to tender and monitor the work to be done; the remote worker must perform to an agreed specification.

After the plan has been proved and tested it should be laid down in a manual for future use. The core managers will also need retraining to learn the techniques of subcontracting work that was previously assigned to fellow employees. Before full-scale implementation, contracts should be drawn up on both sides detailing exactly the rights, duties and obligations of both parties.

Unfortunately, the switch from managing people to briefing consultants has proved too difficult for most managers to accept, which is one reason why this highly imaginative programme has not been adopted more widely. It seems that only a massive change of attitude from board level downwards is likely to show results. Most managers are not prepared to give up direct control of their employees and do not believe that work will be done correctly unless properly supervised. Many feel a loss of status if the numbers reporting to them decline.

Another obstacle is the fact that specifying consultancy contracts, putting these out to tender and monitoring the quality of the results is not part of most management training courses. And communicating with people outside the business is often difficult for managers trained in administration, a problem that has arisen in the subcontracting of local government work.

Regardless of the expected reluctance, the programme has considerable opportunities for two broad categories of people – professionals and those who can work from home through electronic linkages. Suitable professionals include specialized lawyers – those dealing with patents, for example – and accountants working on financial analysis, formulating projects or investigations. Market researchers or marketing specialists, public-relations practitioners, labour-relations and training advisers, security and safety advisers and surveyors and architects are other likely types. So too are stock-market and property analysts, journalists, technical writers, book and magazine editors and copy writers.

Home workers have the image of people operating out of a kitchen or garage, carrying out repetitive manual functions for little return. But, besides helping the professionals, information technology offers a new category of remote worker the possibility of processing information at a remote terminal. British Telecom estimate that some two million people, nearly 10 per cent of the working population, will be working in this way by 1995. They may be processing information, such as company accounts or property prices, or transferring information such as theatre reservations, direct mail addresses or personnel records into a computer system. British Telecom already has an experiment running in

Scotland, in which a number of directory enquiry operators are sited at home, linked to the enquiry computer.

AGENTS FOR CHANGE

Sales agencies have been expanding rapidly in the United States as a way of replacing the fixed expense of a sales or service network with the variable costs of commissions. Individuals work alone or within groups as part of a sales or service organization bought out from the parent to form a new relationship.

The new grouping may enter a fixed contract with their original employers, remaining free to take on other non-competing lines. The method of converting employees to working on commission is similar to the programme for remote working, and it is suitable for sales and service people, merchandisers and those who do customer work of a contracting nature – installers of television aerials, for example.

SHAMROCKS – SUPPLY SPROUTS

The management thinking behind third-generation techniques and shamrock organizations is the same; both rely on the principle of subcontracting work that was previously done in-house. The ideas are not new. From time to time companies have found it more economic to subcontract manufactured items than to produce them internally. What is changing is the nature and scale of the tasks contracted out – they now include such services as cleaning, catering, maintenance, security and computing. But this is just the beginning, and managing a business through debt deflation will require a much greater commitment to this idea. Charles Handy's shamrock organization applies it to the supply, as opposed to the sales, side of the operation.

The symbolism of the shamrock, a structure with three parts, was first mobilized by St Patrick to describe the three aspects of the

Trinity when he was preaching the Gospel to the Irish. On a less exalted level, it provides a useful business metaphor. In Handy's structure, the first leaf represents the core organization, the second represents subcontractors and the third, flexible operators – those that fill the gaps when needed.

Leaf number one is the professional core of an organization, without which the business could not function. It is made up of the essential professionals, technicians and managers who distinguish one business from another. In a sense, they hold the property rights of the company. They are highly paid, well motivated, work exceptionally long hours and are given every inducement to stay with the business. In many Japanese companies, the core consists of 20 per cent of the total shamrock. They know the business backwards and are responsible for initiating and executing (directly or indirectly) all the functions of design, estimating, marketing, subcontracting, quality control and coordination. Managing subcontractors places a high degree of responsibility on managers; in return for strict quality control and reliability, the core must equally strictly honour its promise to pay and work loyally with subcontractors.

Handy believes that the core organization will operate more like a partnership or academic group than the normal pyramid organization, and those involved will expect to be treated like associates, not subordinates. Offices will reflect the changed relationships, being more open plan in design and containing all the associated electronic processing equipment needed for communication and control. The company will be directly connected electronically with subcontractors and clients and, instead of separate offices, will have a number of meeting rooms for executives and associates.

Subcontractors constitute by far the largest part of the shamrock in numbers and are essential to the success of the core.

Their role is to supply the parent with material or expertise under tightly controlled conditions at a specified time. Contractors may operate their own shamrock organizations with associated sub-contractors and flexible workers, and they are likely to be manufacturers, designers or specialist groups who work on a product, hourly or fee basis. They account for 80 per cent of added value in the case of Japanese organizations and may be sited close to the core or be remote according to necessity. One example of low-priority proximity is the County Kerry, Ireland, claims office of an American insurance company.

The essence of second-leaf people or groups (some groups may be quite large) is that they operate under instruction – or licence – from the centre. They are responsible for their own affairs, administrative, organizational and accounting, but they are essentially providers or operators, and their identity is defined by the core or cores for which they work.

The third leaf consists of part-time flexible operators, who make up numbers at particular times of the year. They may be postmen, shop assistants or warehouse packers called in for the Christmas season, for example. They are essential to the first two leaves of the shamrock, because without them the core and sub-contractors could not function efficiently all the year round. Some may be unskilled, finding it is better to have some work in a depression than to be unemployed. Others will be skilled and rated highly by those that take them on; typically, they may have two or three jobs and work highly unusual hours.

SHIRLEY'S SHAMROCK – THE FI GROUP

Very few companies have made shamrock ideas work successfully, though they will have to learn quickly if the business cycles described in chapter 2 progress as expected. Debt deflation is a hard taskmaster; managers will have to learn the techniques of converting fixed to variable costs or go under. There is one company, however, that has been working this way for years – the FI Group.

Based at Hemel Hempstead in Hertfordshire, the FI Group specializes in information technology with its prime accounts in government, industry and commerce. It was started by Steve Shirley in the 1960s, after she left full-time employment as a computer programmer to have a baby. Returning to work as a freelance, she started to win more business than she could handle, and soon she was subcontracting to other freelance people. The idea worked, and it was not until much later that FI employed full-time salaried people. The company has continued to expand, and by 1991 it had sales of nearly £21 million with pre-tax profits of £1.3 million.

The principle of using freelancers has continued – today the company has 300 full-time employees compared with 650 independent professionals who execute contracts under the supervision of project managers. During debt deflation the company will score over its more conventional competitors with its low break-even point. At total fixed costs in 1991 of £7.9 million, the gross margin was over 62 per cent, thus placing the break-even sales level at £12.6 million – or 40 per cent below the sales for the year.

SHAMROCK CROP IN THE PUBLIC SECTOR

Shamrocks have not yet taken much root in private enterprise, so it is ironic that they show every sign of beginning to flourish in the public sector. In the United Kingdom, the Local Government Act of 1988 requires local councils to put out for tender many services that had previously been undertaken by council employees, under a system called compulsory competitive tendering (CTT). The underlying principle of CTT is that outside specialists employing modern management disciplines are likely to provide a better, more cost-effective service than the council's own direct service organizations (DSOs).

Since the Act was passed, councils have prepared tender specifications for local services including refuse collection, building cleaning, grounds maintenance, catering, leisure management, street cleaning and vehicle maintenance. The programme is being extended to cover a range of other services by the end of 1993. Defining the work to be done has not been easy, because so many different services of varying standards have evolved over the course of time. When the contracts were first put out for quotation, the DSOs were invited to tender along with outside contractors and, in many cases, submitted the lowest bid. Problems arose, however, because a number of DSO tenders were not correctly costed and priced, and some of these newly independent groups have since become insolvent.

By mid-1992 contracts to the value of £1.9 billion had been awarded. The largest single category was refuse collection, worth over £500 million, and the smallest, at nearly £80 million, was non-school catering. The results of the first round have been encouraging for the private sector, which had to learn its way through the many complex problems involved in contracting to the public sector. These were some of the reported results.

● **Refuse collection and street cleaning**   Over a quarter of contracts are now held by the private sector – in London, the figure is over 40 per cent. Some of the work has been won by buy-outs, such as MRS Environmental Services, once a part of Westminster City Council, and other successful tenderers include subsidiaries of French and Spanish multinational companies.

● **Building cleaning**   Although the private sector only won 15 per cent of contracts by value, they were awarded the highest number of contracts, with Initial Contract Services emerging as the market leader.

● **School catering**   The private sector finds it difficult to mobilize the resources necessary to manage one school meal a day at widely different locations. The result is that only 3 per cent of contracts went to private firms.

● **Grounds maintenance**   This has been revolutionized by private enterprise, which has introduced mobile teams with specialist equipment to work along a well-planned route. Many firms are involved, including some from Holland and Germany, together with enterprising former DSOs.

● **Vehicle maintenance**   The largest private player is Transfleet Services, a joint venture between the Lex Group and Lombard North Central. Outside contractors provide better vehicle availability than before or are penalized when vehicles are off the road for longer than the agreed downtime periods.

While both councils and private enterprise have had to travel a learning curve, the initial results have been encouraging. Hertfordshire County Council reports that it has saved ratepayers £500,000 on its £3 million ground-maintenance contract. In school cleaning it says it has achieved a 10 per cent financial saving and considerably improved performance levels through use of more modern techniques and higher motivation. The present competition programme is just the start. Many other services are up for consideration, such as the library service, computing and professional services, such as surveying, architecture and legal service. The good news is that the shamrock concept will also be applied to UK central-government services, under the terms of the Citizen's Charter.

ELEVEN

AVOIDING THE CREDIT CRUNCH

The currency crisis of September 1992, when the pound left the European exchange rate mechanism (ERM) and rapidly lost 18 per cent of its value against the Deutschmark, was not Britain's first such upset since World War II. The Attlee government devalued sterling by over 30 per cent against the dollar in September 1949 with little change in interest rates. The Wilson government devalued it by another 14 per cent in November 1967, and this time interest rates rose to nearly 8 per cent in an attempt to hold sterling. Since August 1971, when US President Nixon decoupled the dollar from the gold standard, British interest rates have only been below 9 per cent for relatively short periods – once in 1977 and for brief periods in 1984 and 1988.

With this record of high interest rates and recurring crises, one might have expected British companies to have been somewhat averse to debt. Not a bit of it. Corporate debt nearly doubled from £181 billion in 1985 to £351 billion in 1991, and, although many companies have been reducing their loan exposure under extreme banking pressure, loan interest absorbed 23 per cent of UK corporate income in 1991. As the recession continues to bite, and companies find increasing difficulty in selling their assets for anything like 1990 values, debt interest as a proportion of income is bound to rise.

When the major financial crisis described in chapter 5 arrives, interest rates will start their climb and indebted companies will be the first to suffer from a shortage of capital; too many people will be chasing a diminishing pool of cash. As their cash flow is squeezed, overborrowed businesses will need more money to pay their creditors. The banks, now very cautious after having had so many bad debts and non-performing property loans, will be highly reluctant to throw good money after bad. As the cash pool runs dry, interest rates will rocket.

Consider a hypothetical example of a company that has borrowed extensively to expand but now has to deal with crisis interest rates. It owes the bank £100,000 and is paying interest rates of 10 per cent. In year one, sales are good at £100,00, and margins are sound, giving a profit before interest of £20,000. Interest rates are containable, and, after interest charges of £10,000, the company is left with a pre-tax profit of £10,000. Everyone is happy, and the bank is willing to lend even more.

In year two, however, interest rates have gone up to 15 per cent (a rise of 50 per cent), sales have started to fall, and – since most costs are fixed, regardless of sales – profit margins are being squeezed. Sales ease off to £95,000 and, on the reduced margin, pre-interest profit is down to £15,000. But the interest charge has now risen to £15,000. Pre-tax profits? Nil.

If the company has cash, there are no real problems. There will be time to cut costs and sell assets to fund the borrowings.

Unfortunately, there is no breathing space for those who are already highly borrowed and who need to borrow even more to pay their creditors and buy more stock just to keep trading. They are in a vice. This places the banks in a real quandary. Do they pull the rug now or is there time for the management to take corrective action?

The 'crunch' comes when companies – and individuals – are all starved for cash at the same time and for the same reasons. The cost of money becomes intolerable and the hideous reality dawns – that nothing further can be done but to call a creditors' meeting.

THE RISK IS REAL

Although many companies have taken remedial action since the recession that started in 1990, there are still too many businesses overburdened with debt, as demonstrated by huge private-sector debt levels. In 1992, Syspas, a company performance specialist, reported that 25 per cent of all UK listed industrial and distribution companies were at risk of financial distress. Some of them are large. Syspas noted twelve companies in this category with sales of over £1 billion and forty-seven with sales of between £100 million and £1 billion. Of the total at risk, Syspas rated 1 per cent at 'maximum' risk, implying that there was a high probability of either failure or having to undergo major surgery in the future.

The companies most at risk will be those that borrowed heavily to acquire land – like certain house builders – or conglomerates that made numbers of acquisitions during the 1980s on borrowed money. This is reminiscent of the 1930s, when many large businesses became fit only for dismemberment, while their directors blamed anybody but themselves and pleaded bad luck for their predicament.

Unfortunately, when they go down, these businesses may take others down with them – employees, shareholders, bankers and unsecured creditors. There is little that the government can do to avoid a credit crunch because, like the United States, it has too many other commitments and calls on public cash, though some underwriting of housing and small business will be essential to retain economic and civic stability. The stark reality will be that most businesspeople will have to take responsibility for their own affairs; they will be on their own and can not expect to be bailed out by the government.

PREPARING FOR THE CRUNCH

Those who survive will have understood the sequence of inflation, liquidation and depression explained in chapter 5 and will have made the correct contingency plans. They should also have learnt how to be sound defensive players as did their grandfathers back in the 1930s.

Managing through the mid-1990s will be tough. If the turmoil is as it was in 1931, business will have to cope with rapid swings of interest rates, price gyrations, currency turmoil and indecisive governments. As recommended in the previous chapter, it is essential to appoint a senior director in charge of contingency planning. His job will be to study the likely sequence and understand the leading indicators signalling the turning points of each phase. There could be three months warning of a financial crisis, when the CRB Index referred to in chapter 4 rises above 228 , to prepare sound contingency plans for each stage.

For advance warning of the **inflation** phase, watch the leading indicators for commodity prices and long-dated government securities and then prepare for rising interest rates and raw material prices. Unlike previous inflations, some prices such as commercial property and housing are unlikely to rise; others, such as precious metals, are bound to go up. It would be wise to negotiate flexible pricing for sales but to enter longer contracts for bought-in materials. Towards the peak of the crisis, pay off all available debt, collect whatever cash is owing and reduce inventories to the minimum.

The peak of the crisis will be marked by a fall in commodity prices and easing of interest rates as the pain of the credit crunch becomes too great to bear. This is the **liquidation** phase. Prepare for a rapid run-down of asset values (cash being in very short supply) and a major clamp-down on all forms of spending. This is usually the period when many businesses fail, and cash collection will become a major consideration.

Having survived the crisis and the worst of the liquidation phase, it is then possible to think realistically about the next stage: **depression**. Wise managements will budget for losing one-quarter to one-third of 1990 revenues over a three- to four-year period. Credit will remain extremely tight with limited cash, but in due course fewer companies will fail, and there will be tentative signs of recovery as entrepreneurs bring out new products, new companies are started, and prices stop falling.

There may be several false dawns, but the depth of a depression is an excellent time to negotiate long-term fixed interest loans and long-term supply contracts. Remember, cash will buy good quality assets very cheaply during a recession and enable a business to emerge in healthy condition once credit starts to recover. Remember, it takes more brains to run a business in a recession than in good times and those who succeed will be those who adapt very quickly to changing conditions.

The best defensive position against a credit crunch is to have a low break-even point and to be rich in cash. As argued in chapter 10, managers should first work through the defensive techniques of the normal business cycle. Next they should convert fixed costs to variable costs by adopting third-generation and shamrock organizational structures.

CORRECTING MISMANAGEMENT

There are probably two reasons why many companies will need to take defensive measures to avoid a credit crunch. First, they will have failed to understand – or will have misread – the progress of the business cycles. The majority of the early failures will be those who embarked on major acquisitions or projects on borrowed money, just as a cycle was ending. This is what happened in 1929, 1974, 1980 and is still happening in 1992. Second, they will have made a commercial misjudgement that has either not been detected or has been deliberately concealed.

Commercial misjudgements many take several forms. Companies may have poor control systems, which fail to report accurately where cash is being generated or dissipated. In good times, profits often mask the inadequacy of financial systems. If not put right, indifferent systems are a major cause of failure when times get tough. Overtrading, defined as generating too much volume on too little capital, has also caused many failures. Managements are tempted to generate additional sales on too small a profit margin, particularly when emerging from a recession, and they fail to allow for the rising costs.

Unwise acquisitions and diversifications – particularly if paid for with borrowed money – probably trigger more failures than any other factor. What seems a good idea at the time can rapidly turn sour when the new venture presents technical, accounting or management problems not anticipated when the deal was done. If the difficulties are swept aside and not tackled vigorously, the bad parts often bring down the other, healthy elements of the group. Other examples of mismanagement may be single-produce companies or businesses that are too reliant on one customer. Things can go badly wrong here when previous cosy assumptions are upset in one way or another.

It is most usual to deal with business-cycle recessions by

reducing fixed costs and repaying borrowing by selling surplus assets. But in a debt deflation a second stage is necessary.

STAGE ONE – THE PURGE

What follows is a method for coping with a normal business-cycle recession. The object of stage one is to lower the break-even point by identifying and then disposing of those assets unlikely to be profitable within the next three to five years. The result will be a higher return on a reduced asset base, with cash from disposals paying off debt.

Begin by working out the profitability of the main products or services by division. This will provide a basis for deciding which products and services to keep and which to sell. Most accountants can provide accurate gross profit levels for each activity but few allocate overheads to provide a net figure. Even fewer allocate assets to an activity, which is essential if cash is to be raised for reducing debt.

Select mainstream activities that are readily identifiable at all levels in the business. To each activity allocate direct costs of labour and materials including pensions and social security. Criteria for allocating head-office overheads will vary, depending on the nature of the work. Where an accounting or shipping department is handling a large volume of orders, for example, costs may be allocated by transaction. For others, such as development, the head of the department should make an assessment on the basis of the work done.

Allocating assets is generally more complicated but essential if surplus assets are to be sold for cash to reduce debt. It is easy to allocate inventory when it is identified by product. Other parts of working capital should be considered pro rata; for example, receivables might be divided by the products going to the major accounts. Cash can be netted-off against borrowings and then divided by the working capital held. Finally, allocate fixed assets by usage, occupancy or function, whichever is appropriate. Having drawn up the matrix, now assign each product to one of three categories: holds, sells or possible holds or sells.

Holds These are products that are essential to the business and need to be run as long and as strongly as possible.

Sells These are obvious lossmakers that would need a huge increase in expense to become viable. One marginal product might need a large amount of working capital before it became profitable. Another might need a great deal of development, and others are simply failures.

Possible holds or sells Products that belong in one of the first two categories are relatively easy to recognize. This category holds the products on which opinions are divided and always generates considerable internal argument. It is certain to include pet projects started by senior management, which will never show a profit. An outsider can be a useful adjudicator.

At this point steps should be taken to protect the balance sheet by retaining the value and security of cash, protecting receivables and guarding against inventory obsolescence. A senior executive should be put in charge of implementing the cash-raising and cost-cutting programme, which should be disclosed at an early stage to bankers and certain shareholders (who are not allowed to trade their shares). Once the commercial 'shape' of the business has been agreed and implemented, an inventory reduction programme – such as Just In Time (JIT) deliveries – will reduce stock obsolescence and reduce the inventory for a given sales level even more. The overall effect is to lower the break-even point.

STAGE TWO – RESHAPING THE BUSINESS

Unfortunately, business-cycle defensive measures will not be enough to deal with debt deflation and its dramatic effect on prices and volumes. What will be needed are more drastic methods of lowering the break-even point, described in chapter 10 as third-generation ideas. These usually mean hiving off employees to work on their own – but selling their services back to their previous employers. This might include professional people working from home, sales forces becoming commission-earning agencies and depots or retail outlets becoming independent and working a franchise. Work is either contracted out or licensed by the original parent, and the independent units are free to find additional non-competitive work elsewhere. Such moves will help to prevent running out of cash, by converting fixed costs of company operations to the variable incurring of expenditure only when a sale is made.

It is as well to delay stage two until stage one is complete, as its outcome will determine the activities and supporting staff that need to be retained. Stage-one analysis helps to throw up ideas on what could be hived off, and the subsequent downsizing can mean that what were previously full-time jobs now take up only two or three days a week. Finally, going through stage one usually brings to the surface a whole tier of new leaders who will introduce their own style – not only at the top, but to those lower down the business and to those they bring in.

· IDEAS IN ACTION

Unfortunately, only a few companies will make contingency plans to deal with the forthcoming credit crunch. But they will survive it, whereas the majority, who thought they could muddle through, may find they have left change too late. These ideas take time to implement. But there are companies who have already shown how effective they can be.

THE FOUNDERING FOUNDRY

One of these was a foundry group that had been through four years of marginal trading, culminating in a small pre-tax loss. Its net worth was declining, and its situation was potentially terminal. The business operated from five locations and relied on two major accounts that had reduced their orders.

A new chief executive was appointed, and he undertook a stage-one analysis. The main plants were in the West Midlands, the North-East and London. Another factory, in Dudley, made bathroom fittings and had an uneconomical plating plant. When the larger contracts were analysed it appeared that 80 per cent of the income was coming from 25 per cent of the customers. The remaining 75 per cent of the accounts were either too small or had been taken on at marginal profitability.

The solution was based on the principle of concentration. Work on all major contracts was brought to the Midlands, and money was spent on improving dies, tooling and machinery to increase margins. Production of certain products was terminated by disposal to third parties. There was also a sale of surplus plant.

The foundry in the North-East had assets of some £2 million operating at a loss. It was decided to transfer plant and working capital worth £1 million to the Midlands and to sell the balance to the foundry's general manager for a small sum. The plating work at the Dudley factory was subcontracted out more economically. Bathroom product manufacture was transferred to the Midlands and the plant sold. The small London plant suffered the same fate.

The following year, operations were profitable despite lower sales, and the cash raised from the asset sales was used to pay outstanding bills and reduce the overdraft. The number of employees fell from 1800 to 1100, and the efficiency of the company was improved as its output per employee increased by nearly 20 per cent. The recovery continued in subsequent years, and the increase in cash flow was ploughed back into the business with the purchase of new automatic foundry equipment.

GLASS-FABRICATION FRANCHISEES

A specialist glass company supplying hi-tech products to science-based manufacturers and to the trade was profitable, but investors had not given the business a good rating because of its unpredictable performance. Fearing the onset of a recession, a small group of shareholders encouraged the company to enrol a non-executive director who had experience with profit improvement programmes. It was proposed that he would work with the executives with the aim of improving the uneven profit record and strengthening the balance sheet.

It was with some reluctance that the board accepted the newcomer; after all, the company was profitable and how could an outsider possibly understand a business that the directors had taken decades to master? The view of the chairman eventually prevailed; he was a sizeable shareholder in his own right and had been concerned about the lack of stock-market acceptance.

The new director recommended stage-one analysis to discover the trading strengths and weaknesses of the company. He insisted that the work should be done by executives on the principle that they would believe and implement the results if they did the analysis themselves. The auditors could provide financial help.

The products were divided into five groups – rods, fabrication, special projects, moulded products and 'other'. It appeared the erratic profit record was caused almost entirely by an uneven offtake of a very few customers who bought the special project products. The work was so profitable that when demand was good overall performance was excellent; when it was poor, the losses from fabrication and 'other' pulled the company down and made it vulnerable to a take-over.

The resulting recommendations were that the profitable rods and moulded products groups required little change, though a minimum rods order size was suggested. It was also recommended that rods sales to small customers should be passed to distributors, with some administrative savings. Special projects was left untouched. Most of the lines in the 'other' category (many of which were pet projects) were dropped, in spite of the outcry from their sponsors.

The loss-making fabrication group was an excellent franchising opportunity, however. The production director reluctantly agreed that the skills could be mastered in a few weeks with instruction by his specialized team. He also agreed that some of his plant could be sold to the franchisees, providing that some skills and equipment were kept within the company. There were labour overhead savings to be made, but many of the skilled men were redeployed as franchisees or trainers.

It was estimated that if the programme had been implemented from day one of that year, profits by year four would have been boosted by around 50 per cent. This took into account the loss of contribution by 'other' products and an 18-month gestation period for franchising fabrication. In the longer term, franchising fabrication would add at least a further 25 per cent to profits.

TAKING OUT TILE COSTS

A tile manufacturer had been doing excellent business but faced growing competition and was anxious to prepare for recession. Its products were decorated tiles for interior walls, floors and patios, sold mainly to builders merchants and directly to specialist shops and larger stores. The clay was bought, shaped, fired and then decorated with transfers before being glazed, packed and shipped to distributors. The competition was coming from specialists selling personalized tiles at a considerable premium. The company's leading indicators showed that the recession was already hitting sales and that there would not be a sizeable upturn until 1994–5. Action was needed.

An analysis of the business showed that while the number of products and designs had proliferated during the boom years, their lack of profitability was masked by good margins on the major lines. It also revealed many direct small accounts opened by specialist stores, which were costly to service despite their higher margins. The overheads were being skewed towards the specialist business. Finally, it was estimated that a volume/price decline of some 30 per cent was quite likely in the main markets over a two-year period and that this would push the business firmly into loss.

A small management group was set up to consider options for the specialist work. This was a growth business but required small production teams producing a plethora of uneconomical batches. As individual demand was difficult to forecast, so the stocks of specialist tiles were expanding, and it was increasingly expensive to ship small quantities. The working party suggested that the finishing operation could be undertaken by franchisees. They would be supplied with unfinished blanks, together with a large selection of transfers. When they received an order, a small batch would be made up and shipped, so keeping the company's specialized inventory at a minimum.

The franchisees would buy some of the small batch kilns and take responsibility for their own inventory and sales ledger. The company would sell other fixed assets at book value and be left to concentrate on its major business, so reducing direct and indirect costs. The results of a feasibility study showed that direct costs fell faster than sales, and there were other savings in marketing and administration. Some of the money saved on costs was switched to development, where expenditure was tripled. Overall, profit on sales increased by 100 per cent and sales per employee by 22 per cent. Much of the company's borrowings could be paid back by cash raised from asset sales, and the break-even point was reduced by some 36 per cent.

STAYING IN TOUCH

In any exercise, like the ones described above, timing and communication are important, and there are some tips to be borne in mind.

● There will be a lot of speculation and rumour while any evaluation is taking place, so it would be wise to have the results within three months of starting, or the best people will start to leave.

● Use highflyers to lead the analytical teams because they will also be responsible for implementing the changes and then running the new departments.

● The products or services identified as 'holds' will often need new departmental groupings with different people in charge. This could be a good opportunity for promotion from within.

● Good communication is essential if the work is to go smoothly. The workforce should be kept closely in touch with the objectives and implementation of the plan once it is agreed. Customers will need to be reassured of continuing supply, and should be encouraged to switch products from discontinued lines. Suppliers should also be informed if the business mix changes.

● Bankers should be certainly kept informed of the cash-flow programme and asked to provide bridging loans if necessary. In some cases, a committee of institutional shareholders is appointed to stay abreast of the programme, on the strict understanding that their information is confidential and they are treated as insiders – and so may not trade shares on the basis of this information. Alternatively, it would be wise to arrange briefing meetings with the major shareholders once the changes have been announced.

TWELVE

AN EDGE FOR INVESTORS

Investors will be faced with a roller-coaster of inflation, credit collapse and depression as the cycle moves to its crisis and beyond. It will be difficult enough to maintain capital values, let alone make profits in any currency, unless investors have a strategy that takes into account each phase of the crisis. Remember that anyone holding General Motors stock before the 1929 crash did not see the share price at similar levels until 1952. For some investors, painful memories are somewhat fresher – anyone holding fixed-interest stock during the inflation of 1973-4 saw their capital values collapse.

It is important that UK investors, even those who do not dabble in international stocks, keep a close eye on the US economy. It is still the world's largest, and the dollar is the world's reserve currency, in which substantial trade is conducted, and most commodities are priced. What happens in the United States will be felt by investors all over the world.

In chapter 5 it was suggested that the tightening vice of high debt and changing weather could give rise to three scenarios for the American economy. The first was a controlled return to balanced budgets and currency stability; the second was continuing debt deflation; and the third foresaw a vicious inflationary spike before a collapse into a deep depression. Investment strategy for the first two scenarios is relatively straightforward and is dealt with only briefly. The third, and worst, scenario demands the ability to think ahead, act fast and change tactics for each stage of the crisis.

Scenario one envisages a controlled return to a virtuous spiral of balanced budgets and stable currencies. This would demand politicians with the courage drastically to reduce public spending and return currencies to the stern discipline of a commodity standard such as gold. If this were to happen, excellent investments would again be found in fixed-interest stocks and precious metals that would immediately regain value as a means of exchange.

In scenario two – the 'business as usual' scenario – the politicians behave as if this were just another recession and so precipitate a replay of the 1930s. There would be a gradual decline into depression, and then a slow return of credit while lenders and borrowers regained trading confidence. Like the 1930s, the best investments are likely to be government stock or fixed-interest commercial bonds in rock-solid companies.

INVESTING THROUGH THE CRISIS AND BEYOND

The third and most likely scenario predicts soaring inflation while governments attempt to maintain their spending. There will then be a comprehensive credit collapse and depression. As prudent investors should have contingency plans for a worst-case scenario, this possibility is described in more detail.

INFLATION – BONDS OUT, RESOURCE STOCKS IN

The squeeze between high commodity prices and swelling debt will cause intolerable pressure on the authorities who will be forced to 'accommodate' by flooding the market – and particularly the banks – with cash. This would be not unlike the 'dash for growth' of the Conservative administration in the early 1970s. The signals now, as then, would be increasing raw-material prices, a collapse in the bond market, a rising stock-market, a rise in the cost of living index and eventually a rise in short-term interest rates.

The most indebted nations, such as the United States, Britain and perhaps Japan, would be the first to initiate inflation. As the US has the largest traded bond and commodity market, probably the best indicator would be the T-bond yield rising above 9.5 per cent and the price of gold rising above $360 per ounce. Other markets would almost certainly follow the United States.

The following moves have been found to be sound strategies in past inflations. However, care should be taken because it is quite possible that governments, in a revived form of economic national-ism, would impose exchange controls, so preventing people from converting cash into other currencies.

Fixed-interest securities would not be a good investment and should be sold as early as possible, once it was evident that the inflation phase had started. Yields would start to rise as buyers of stocks demanded a higher return to protect themselves from declining currency values. Some equities will respond to inflation – defensive stocks, such as food processing and utilities (water and electricity), and resource stocks, such as mining and oil, for example. British index-linked stocks would also do well.

Eurodollar interest rate futures could be a good hedge against declining currency values, particularly for international-based portfolios. A sound strategy in Germany during the early 1920s was to borrow in a currency that is likely to decline and buy casily held and easily liquidated commodities, such as gold or silver. At some point in the inflationary spiral, the holding can be sold, and the loan repaid at a value below the borrowing price. This game gets increasingly dangerous if governments force up interest rates to protect their currency.

Soft traded commodities, such as wheat, soya beans, sugar and corn, should move upwards quite rapidly, but unless investors have arrangements to trade these in futures markets, they may find it difficult to accommodate contract sizes of 5000 bushel of wheat. If inflation becomes dramatic, as it did in Germany during the early 1920s, then base metals such as copper, lead and zinc will also rise in price even though the underlying recession is restricting demand for raw materials. Regardless of the severity of the rise in inflation, now is the time to be holding physical gold.

LIQUIDATION – OUT OF RESOURCES, BACK TO (SOUND) BONDS

The inflation phase could start in 1993, take a little while to become established then accelerate to a peak in 1994, by which time the pain will be extreme. Interest rates in the United States could be well over 25 per cent, and, with bond yields around 20 per cent, government borrowing will become prohibitively expensive. As politicians are forced to pull back heavily on expenditure – much more heavily than if they had adopted a scenario-one strategy – the reins of government will be loosened. One tell-tale sign of this condition will be the plummeting of the Federal Reserve Credit figure. At this point the central bank will no longer be able to raise further credit and a fully fledged credit collapse will have begun.

It will be terrible for those relying on government employment or spending; it will be just as bad for companies, individuals and investors holding government securities. Just as anyone holding German government securities in 1924 lost almost everything, those now owning the $4 trillion US government debt will be similarly bereft. Debt will become extremely unpopular. Any form of surplus asset – houses, securities, companies, jewellery, works of art – will be sold in a mad scramble for liquidity. This will not be the end of America or other countries in a similar condition; after a period of trauma and upheaval there will be a rebuilding of society from the bottom upwards; and the role of government will be redefined. There is a huge degree of resilience in advanced countries, as Germany showed after the crash in the early 1920s and again, with Japan, after World War II.

Technically, the point at which inflation ends and liquidation begins may not be easy to judge because politics could still fudge the issue. During the run-up to the 1980 presidential election, for example, the rapid reduction of short-term interest rates had probably more to do with the incumbent Jimmy Carter wanting to be re-elected than the underlying state of the economy and bond market. However, accompanying the crisis peak will be a rapid fall in commodity prices as these are sold for liquidity. Bond and bill yields will also collapse as, quite suddenly, nobody can afford to borrow any more. The trick, as always, is to pre-empt the turn, but not by too much. The catch is that those who miss the turn many find they have a long way to fall. If it is still possible to invest outside one's own country, strategy should include some of the following elements.

Buy long-term bonds in a country not so prone to possible currency devaluation. This might well suggest Swiss government or corporate bonds, for example. Sell equities that are not part of essential long-term core holdings. Sell commodities – their price should fall rapidly in the general scramble for liquidity. At least part of the gold portfolio should be held, however, in case of currency collapse.

The liquidation phase is generally shorter than the inflation phase. Note that at this point it becomes difficult to trade at all because the exchanges will themselves be under tremendous pressure, and many of them will cease operating. If the stock-market remains open, the end of the liquidation phase is the time to pick up some cheap longer term quality recovery stocks.

DEPRESSION – INTO RECOVERY STOCKS

The liquidation phase ends with a collapse in the value of assets and paper securities in the worst affected countries. Cash is 'king' and in very short supply, to the extent that barter systems will spring up. It will be a period of immense change and of considerable unrest and instability. Investment will not be easy until some life stirs in the economy, and credit starts rebuilding. However, when disposable income does start rising, stocks in stores, insurance, banks and building material should rise rapidly, and there could be strong upward moves in the stock-markets generally.

PICKING AND CHOOSING

What follows is a list of firms divided between resource and recovery stocks. It should be stressed that these are in no sense recommendations to buy any particular stock, but rather illustrations of the types of business whose shares may outperform in different phases of a financial crisis.

RESOURCE STOCKS – UP WITH INFLATION

Asarco (US) is primarily a copper producer, with interests in lead, zinc, silver and industrial minerals and a range of international holdings.

Freeport McMoran (US) produces copper, gold, sulphur, oil and gas; it may refine 550,000 ounces of gold in 1992.

Inco (Canada) is the world's largest nickel producer and also mines copper, silver and platinum.

Newmont Mining (US) produces coal and around 1.5 million ounces of gold each year. Sir James Goldsmith owns 49.1 per cent of the equity.

Phelps Dodge (US) is the largest US copper producer, refiner and fabricator.

Burlington Resources (US) is the leading independent natural-gas producer in the United States. Energy stocks have been relatively low key during the mild winters of 1990-1, but this could change with a period of cooler, drier weather.

Western Mining (Australia) is one of Australia's largest resource companies with interests including gold, nickel, alumina, copper and oil. It was started during the 1930s depression and has overseas interests in Canada, the United States and Brazil.

RTZ (UK) is the world's largest mining company, producing copper, gold, aluminium, iron, lead, zinc and other metals. The company has substantial mining interests around the globe, notably in the United States.

Bank of International Settlements (Switzerland) in Basle is banker to many of the world's central banks, twenty-nine of which are also shareholders. However, 16 per cent of its equity is still traded. Gold forms a large proportion of the assets and for every $1 increase in the price of gold, its net assets increase by an estimated SFr8 million, or SFr17 per share.

RECOVERY STOCKS – AFTER THE FALL

Hornbach (Germany) is a do-it-yourself store, which has more than doubled its sales since 1987. Since opening its first store in 1968, it has overtaken bigger groups by offering a wider range of merchandise than its competitors. It has since moved into the larger cities in east Germany. Stores such as these should perform well even in a depression.

Northumbrian Water (UK) is one of the newly privatised utilities likely to benefit if the changing weather described in chapter 3 results in water shortages. Although much of the business is still tightly regulated, 20 per cent of the group's earnings come from waste management and environmental engineering.

Degremont (France) is a world leader in the production, installa tion and management of water-treatment plants both for public services and industrial recycling of waste water. The company nearly failed in the early 1980s but was rescued by Lyonnaise des Eaux-Dumez, which holds 88 per cent of the stock. The company has considerable international business, which should stand it in good stead as water becomes an increasingly expensive commodity.

Orsan (France) is the only biotechnology share listed on the Paris Bourse. It specializes in the production of amino acids, the essential input for adding protein to animal feed, and in glutamate, an amino-acid additive for human consumption often used to flavour food. Orsan should do well in any animal-feed shortage, as described in chapter 9.

Lapeyre (France) is the uncontested leader in the manufacture of industrial joinery in France, and it stands to do well should investment in housing refurbishment increase during the recession.

Serco (UK) is a management company specializing in running non-core services for public corporations. The company's prime growth is in the UK public sector, particularly with the local authorities. Private-sector accounts include British Steel, Marks and Spencer and British Aerospace. It should do well as the shamrock management philosophy described in chapter 10 develops.

Damart (France), the specialist cool-weather clothing manufacturer and retailer, has had a poor patch during the above-average temperatures of recent years. Changing weather patterns are likely to prompt a return to cooler, drier winters.

Kurita Water Industries (Japan) makes specialized water-treatment plant and radioactive waste-treatment equipment. It has recently moved into environmental equipment and biotechnology.

Japan Organo (Japan) is somewhat smaller than Kurita and specializes in ultra-pure water for nuclear power, semiconductor production and for plastics, chemicals and other processes.

Secom (Japan) has around 60 per cent of Japan's alarm and electronic security systems market. It also makes more high-tech items, such as sensors, and has subsidiaries in the United States. This is a large business with sales of Y172,000 million and profits of nearly 14 per cent of sales.

Sakata Seed (Japan) is the largest seed company in eastern Japan. The company is strong in genetic research and sells through merchants and horticultural stores. It has a US subsidiary.

Honen (Japan) is a company, not unlike Orsan, processing edible oils for animal feed, health foods and fine chemicals. It is the second largest of its kind in Japan in terms of market share.

Hewlett-Packard (US) is likely to be a beneficiary as more people work from home. The company is a leading producer of personal computers and laser and ink-jet printers – ideal for individuals producing high quality documentation.

Groundwater Technology (US) is a leading provider of turnkey groundwater clean-up and restoration services. The groundwater present in aquifers provides around 50 per cent of all the drinking water in the United States, and the company's technology will make more available in times of diminishing rainfall.

US Surgical Corporation (US) is the world's largest manufacturer of surgical staplers, with a substantial share of the world 'wound closure' market. It would stand to benefit from increasing concern with efficient healthcare.

McGraw-Hill (US) is a world leader in educational publications and associated material. It is likely to benefit from an increasing demand for retraining in the western world, as many are required to learn new skills or set up on their own.

THIRTEEN

AFTER THE STORM

The Great Depression of the 1990s will end, as it must, and a new recovery will begin. A fresh Juglar cycle will gather steam, and yet another Kondratieff begin its slow ascent to the peak. Credit and investment will grow again, and the world economy will start to emerge from its metaphoric shelter. The bad times will fade, leaving only tales to be retold and lessons, in due course, to be forgotten. And yet people and society, businesses and governments will never be quite the same again.

The depression will not have brought about the change on its own – it will merely have accelerated a process, a swinging of the pendulum, that was already under way. But the fact remains that its trying conditions will have encouraged a new self-reliance and sense of independence that will affect people's attitudes towards themselves, their families and communities and their local and central authorities.

For millions, reliance on the security provided by a large employer and the helping hand of government will be a thing of the past. Businesses will be obliged to adapt themselves for survival either by simple and savage retrenchment, accompanied by large-scale redundancies, or by more forward-looking reshaping into third-generation and shamrock structures, employing the latest cybernetic techniques. As its revenues shrink and demands for assistance increase, government will simply no longer be able to afford the full panoply of the welfare state.

The result will be that more and more people will be thrown back on their own resources and on those of their families and communities with, possibly, an accompanying revival in good manners, fellowship and faith. Self-help will be the order of the day, an experience some will find more exhilarating than others. Unfortunately, many will suffer greatly, and the pressures will be enough to break up some families. Others may find that their ties are strengthened as a result. Indeed, the much derided nuclear family many well stage a comeback, as more family businesses are established. These are likely to involve not only those family members of working age but also parents, grandparents – who will be living longer at the same time as birthrates are falling – and children who will grow up with the business.

Some commentators believe that 50 per cent of the working population will be either self-employed or working in small groups by 1995. While the retreat of government and big business will provide the impetus, technology is already in place to provide the means for this to happen. Computers, satellite communications, fax machines and cellular phones all combine to free people from the need to go to where the work is – the work can follow them to wherever it suits them to be, whether they operate from home or an office location of their own choosing. Many will opt to leave the cities and move to more rural areas. Some may even choose to live in another country, if this suits their personal or tax circumstances.

Changes in the working environment will be accompanied by changes in lifestyle. Higher food prices will prompt closer attention to cheap but sustaining food. Eating out will become a luxury. With cash in short supply during the depression, barter systems may enjoy a revival. A model already operates in Courtenay, British Columbia, where local people offer their skills in exchange for a credit recorded on a central computer. The credit can then be used to buy from another member of the system.

People will also travel less. For those working from home, there will be no need to commute. Even for those with their own offices, technology will reduce the necessity for and the frequency of face-to-face meetings. And, at least in the early years of the depression, the need to be careful with money will make people think twice about undertaking journeys.

As people emerge from the culture of dependence, their attitudes towards government and its role in their lives will change. For its own part, government will be obliged to reassess and adapt its relationship with voters and taxpayers, both on a political and on an administrative level. People, discovering that they are actually rather proficient at running their own lives, will start to resent excessive government interference. Instead of paying high taxes in order that central government may decide how the money should be allocated, they will want to retain more of their own earnings and decide how to spend it themselves – particularly in areas such as health and education. And there will be enough of them who think this way for political parties seriously to have to address their needs and desires. The lobbying power of trades unions, the Confederation of British Industry and the Institute of Directors will be diluted, as their constituencies shrink. The government will suffer an equal and opposite reduction in its power to use these lobbies as an economic lever.

Government will also have to adapt itself to a fragmentation in its revenue base. In the early 1980s nearly 90 per cent of taxpayers were in full-time employment. They contributed their taxes in a conveniently steady stream via the pay-as-you-earn (PAYE) system, claimed no value added tax (VAT) rebates and enjoyed very little in the way of allowable deductions from taxable income. In a depression and post-depression economy, the number of these full-time employees will shrink dramatically. They will be replaced by many who opt to become Schedule D (sole trader) taxpayers, submitting their returns at the end of the financial year and deducting their business expenses from their taxable income. Many will become VAT-registered and so claw back VAT spent on supplies. All this will have the effect of further reducing government's income and its scope for spending.

People who work for themselves or in small groups generally feel a greater sense of responsibility to the task at hand than those submerged in large organizations. They pay close attention to quality and output, because they have to – their livelihood, in a very direct sense, depends on it. This in itself will contribute strongly to the recovery and a resumption of the upwards trend in the economic cycle.

But there is another, overarching cycle at work. Raymond Wheeler, whose research was described in chapter 3, charted the development and character of societies in terms of prevailing climate. He found that cool and dry periods of history encouraged the growth of independence, as human energies were stimulated, and people shook off their oppressors. These, he said, were dynamic times, accompanied by a return to the fundamentals of ethics and basic values. He predicted that the 1990s would be such a period. If he were right, we all have something to look forward to.

POSTSCRIPT

The Western world is still poised between collapsing into a deflationary vortex or being sucked into an inflationary spiral – the two alternative scenarios described in chapter 5 of *Meltdown*. Since the original manuscript was completed in October 1992, each possibility has come into sharper forcus.

The world seems to function in 60-year cycles, which is why the history of the deflationary 1930s has such a familiar ring today. Will we really have to live through the same events once again? Recessions make countries very nationalistic; because of this, the French farming lobby could still force their government to demand special treatment, thus aborting the Uruguay Round trade talks – just like the American farmers forced President Hoover to sign the Smoot Hawley Act in June 1931. As in the 1930s, the world could be plunged into protectionism. Politicians were held in poor regard in the 1930s, just as they are now. The Conservatives, forming the bulk of the UK National Government, were known as the 'stupid party' and the opposition were just as insipid and bereft of ideas as they are 60 years later. In the United States, George Bush fought the 1992 election on similar grounds to Herbert Hoover in 1932 – both lost. Unfortunately, Bush's successor has neither the style nor the spending power that Franklin Roosevelt commanded when elected president in 1932.

Fortunately, Europe has escaped dictatorships – so far. Neither Italy or Germany seems likely to become fascist in the near future, although Italy could divide into north and south and a deepening recession could still break up Germany. However, the real danger comes from Russia. This huge country could collapse into anarchy – and possibly famine – just as in every country that has allowed hyper-inflation to prevail. Britain cannot afford to be smug; the first successor to Sir Oswald Mosley's Blackshirts was elected to the Tower Hamlets council in September 1993, and, given encouragement, Scotland could secede from Britain – not unlike the 1930s when the Scottish National Party was led by the Duke of Montrose. Britain ran down its armed services during the 1930s, believing there was no threat – and paid for it. We could be doing the same now.

At least in the 1930s people were not living way beyond their means. Now almost every Western nation is running a huge deficit as politicians, despite falling tax revenue, attempt to continue spending in the hope of engineering a recovery. As the Americans are discovering, this is difficult despite the lowest interest rates for decades. When countries are in a credit vortex, the only sensible response is to organize a credit back-up – as Roosevelt discovered in 1933.

It is this massive rise in debt that encourages one to suspect that in the end inflation will win. Of the Western nations, the Belgians have the largest government debt to gross national product (debt/GNP ratio) at 130%, closely followed by Italy with 110%; the Americans are not far behind at nearly 70%, while Britain's stands at 45%. Most debt is rising fast and therein lies the problem, because governments have to pay interest which increasingly swallows up taxed revenue. They then have two choices: either they can default or defraud their creditors by allowing a currency collapse. Both have their problems.

In the 1930s, Germany defaulted on their debt interest, which forced Britain off the Gold Standard in September 1931 – just 61 years before the UK left the ERM in September 1992. Germany was followed by Mexico which, in September 1933, could no longer service its loans; Brazil then threw in the towel in 1937. Debt default is never popular. It makes it very hard for the country to raise credit in the future.

The other way of reducing debt is to make it valueless, as Germany proved in 1924. The government had gone on literally printing money in the hope of keeping up their spending, but the failing mark kept ahead of the printing presses and spending was only possible with ever higher denomination notes. The German savers, who had paid for the war effort, had bought government securities but were left holding worthless paper.

Apart from debt, food prices could be rising again due to the extraordinary weather in many parts of the globe in 1993 – probably continuing to 1994. The governments' alternatives are depressing: should they clamp down on inflation and make everyone poorer or print money to keep down interest rates? *Meltdown* maintains either would be the way of weak governments – akin to pouring paraffin on a fire. It would lead to rocketing interest rates and commodity prices before many Western economies collapsed into a depressionary vortex.

But *Meltdown* is optimistic. Mankind has been through worse fixes before and will undoubtedly come through the 1990s, though not in the way many expect. One of the cycles described in this book works over 500 years, suggesting that there will be a switch of productive capacity from the West to the East as developed countries, burdened with high levels of on-costs, are less able to compete in world markets. This is already happening; firms are now finding it more economical to manufacture in the newly industrializing countries around the Western Pacific rim than in their own countries.

The impact on jobs and the ability of Western governments could be profound. As fewer people can look forward to full-time employment, those without work will receive less state support as the downturn forces reluctant politicians to cut back on government spending. Those obliged to become self-employed will either have to work independently or in small groups, and many will prosper acting as sub-contractors for larger corporations. Although life could be uncomfortable for a time, people will emerge tougher and more resilient to taste a high degree of freedom as individuals take more responsibility for their own lives.

FURTHER READING

Aldcroft, Derek H., *The British Economy Between the Wars* (Philip Allen), 1983.

Beckman, Robert, *The Downwave: Surviving the Second Great Depression* (Milestone), 1983.

Browning, Iben and Winkless, Nels III, *Climate and the Affairs of Men* (Fraser), 1975.

Cohen, Stan, *The Tree Army: A Pictorial History of the Civilian Conservation Corps, 1933–1942* (Pictorial Histories), 1980.

Davidson, James Dale and Rees-Mogg, Lord William, *The Great Reckoning* (Sidgwick & Jackson), 1992.

Duijn, Van J.J., *The Long Wave in Economic Life* (Allen & Unwin), 1983.

Fergusson, Adam, *When Money Dies* (William Kimber), 1975.

Figgie, Harry E. with Swanson, Gerald J., *Bankruptcy, 1995: The Coming Collapse of America and How to Stop It* (Little, Brown), 1992.

Handy, Charles, *The Age of Unreason* (Century Hutchinson), 1989.

Houston, William and Lewis, Nigel, *The Independent Director: Handbook and Guide to Corporate Governance* (Butterworth Heinemann), 1992.

Howell, Ralph, *Why Not Work? A Radical Solution to Unemployment* (Adam Smith Institute), 1991.

Johnson, Paul, *A History of the Modern World from 1917 to the 1980s* (Weidenfeld & Nicholson), 1983.

Lamb, H. H., *Climate History and the Modern World* (Methuen), 1982.

Landsheidt, Theodor, *Sun-Earth-Man: A Mesh of Cosmic Oscillations* (Urania Trust), 1988.

McElveine, Robert, *The Great Depression: America, 1929–1941* (Times Books), 1984.

Sloan, Alfred P. Jr, *My Years with General Motors* (Pan), 1963.

St Etienne, Christian, *The Great Depression, 1929–1938* (Hoover Press), 1986.

Stoskoof, Neil, *Cereal Grain Crops* (Reston), 1984.

Toffler, Alvin, *The Third Wave* (Pan), 1981.

Wright, Celia, *The Wright Diet* (Grafton), 1986.

Zahorchak, Michael, *Climate: The Key to Understanding Business Cycles* (Tide Press), 1983.

INDEX

Acts of Confinement, 98
Adolphus, Gustavus, 33
agency, 166
agriculture
  cereals, 138–45
  cooling, effect of, 135–6
  corn, 141–3
  grain for animals, 146
  grains, 136–7
  land removed from, 32
  meat, 145–7
  oats and barley, 144–5
  rice, 136–7, 143–4
  rye, 140
  triticale, 141
  wheat, 138–40
American Civil War, 18, 55
Asama, eruption of, 28
assets
  liquidation of, 68
  personal, study of, 93
  assignat, 69, 70
Austria
  inflation scenario, 72–3
  state employees, 73

bank failures, 37–8
barter systems, 201
Blum, Léon, 4, 65–6
Bolger, Jim, 88
Bonaparte, Napoleon, 34, 70
boom/crisis/recession/recovery cycle, 7
Bosnia, war in, 47
Britain, dry period in, 40
British banks
  September 1931, run on, 38
British Trust for Conservation
  Volunteers (BTCV), 107–9, 111, 113,
  117
Browning food cycle, 11
  grain harvests, prognosis for, 32
  Kondratieff cycle, relationship with,
  32
  sunspots, effect of, 31–3
  tidal trigger, 29–30
Browning, Iben, 28–32

building projects
  return, not showing, 8
Bush, George, 40, 43, 64
business
  agency, 165
  crunch, preparing for, 176–7
  downsizing, 159
  franchising, 160–2, 183–5
  managing, 153
  purging, 179–80
  recovery management, 157–9
  remote working, 163–6
  retail or wholesale outlets, releasing,
    160
  shamrock organizations, 160, 166–71
  third generation, approach, 159
business cycles, low point of, 3
Business Expansion Scheme (BES), 92
business-cycle recession
  business, reshaping, 181
  central bankers, responses of, 45
  contingency ideas in action, 182–6
  coping with, 179–81
  demand-led recovery, 44
  holds and sells, 180
  investment in, 189
  managing, 153–4
  standard of living, maintenance of,
    44–5
  staying in touch, 186–7
  survival, adaptation for, 199–200

capital gains tax
  abolition, proposed, 87
cattle, 147
central Europe
  famine, prospect of, 4
central government, role of, 3
Chamberlain, Neville, 38, 58
China
  agriculture, land removed from, 32
  grain drain, 136
Civil Works Administration (CWA), 63,
  98
Civilian Conservation Corps (CCC), 63,
  97–8, 103–7, 113, 116

Civilian Environmental Corps (CEC), 113–17
climatic change, 2, 4
  agriculture, and. *See* Agriculture
  business conditions, alteration of, 21
  cool/dry periods, 35
  crop yields, affecting, 22
  effects of, 135
  food shortages, and, 23
  grain shortfall, creating, 147–8
  maximum cooling, 136
  thousand-year cycle, 34–6
  volcanic eruptions, effect of, 24–9
  warm/wet periods, 35
Clinton, Bill, 40, 43, 56, 84, 93–4
Commodity Research Bureau (CRB) Index
  commodity prices, measuring, 47, 51–2
  critical level, 67
  volcanic activity, indicator of, 52–3
Commonwealth of Independent States (CIS)
  agriculture, land removed from, 32
  civil war and rebellions in, 19
  economy of, 46
  grain drain, 136
  Islamic fundamentalism, 47
  tensions in, 46
community service
  introduction of, 112–13
  projects, planning, 114–16
compulsory competitive tendering (CTT), 85, 169–71
Cosiguina, eruption of, 28
Council of Mortgage Lenders (CML), 125–6
credit
  crunch, preparing for, 176–7, 181
  debt mushroom, 42–5
  excess, getting rid of, 5
  trust, based on, 5
  vortex, 9
Creditanstalt, guarantee of debts, 37
crisis
  Juglar cycle, phase of, 12

Darby, Abraham, 16
debt

companies at risk, 175–6
consumer, level of, 43
corporate, level of, 173–5
gross public, 93–4
monetizing, 67
partial repayments, 128
stay of execution, advantage of, 128
writing off, 42
debt deflation, 9–10
  business management in, 153
  business, reshaping, 181
  keeping company profitable, 159
  recovery management, 157–9
debt inflation, 9, 44
defence installations, closure of, 86
depression
  after the storm, 199–202
  charity, lack of, 4
  current and 1930s compared, 39–42
  inflation and liquidation, following, 68
  investment in, 194
  long-term loans, negotiation of, 177
  people, caused by, 1
  preparation for, 177
devaluation, 173
dictatorship, 3
downwave, 9–10
Drummond, Sir Jack, 149

economic and climatic cycles
  Browning food cycle, 11. *See also* Browning food cycle
  convergence of, 10
  effects, predicting, 10
  eighteen-year Kuznets real-estate cycle, 11. *See also* Kuznets cycle
  human behaviour, determined by, 21
  Kondratieff cycle, 11. *See also* Kondratieff cycle
  low points, at, 8
  managing, 154–6
  nine-to-eleven-year Juglar cycle, 10. *See also* Juglar cycle
  thousand-year, 34–6
  Wheeler cycle, 11
  180-year sun-retrograde cycle, 11, 33–4
economists

climatic matters, ignorance of, 22
education
  costs, cutting, 87–8
  efficient running of, 90
  New Zealand, in, 87–9
  transfer of cost, 87
European Community, defaults within, 40
Exchange Rate Mechanism (ERM)
  British withdrawal from, 39, 173
  departure from gold standard, events reminiscent of, 39
  Italian devaluation within, 38–9
exchange rates
  overvalued currency, for, 63

Federal Deposit Insurance Scheme (FDIC), 131
Federal Reserve Credit
  indicator, as, 47
  bond yields and consumer prices, relationship with, 50
  Federal Reserve System, measure of credit in, 50
Federal Savings and Loans Insurance Corporation (FSLIC), 131–2
Fergusson, Adam, 78
Figgie, Harry, 86
financial crisis
  American recovery, 1930s, 59–63
  business-as-usual scenario, 63–4
  contingency plans for, 81
  entrepreneurs, role of, 82
  experience of, 56
  government power, cutting back on, 82
  painful cutbacks in, 56–7
  public expenditure, pruning, 58
  public spending, cutbacks in, 82–4
  short-term interest rates, raising, 57
  survival briefings, 55
  survival coalition government, 1931, 58–9
  traditional government response, 55
  triggers for action, 57
fixed costs, changing to variable, 85
food
  average consumption, 149–50
  corn, 141–3

growth, requirements for, 23–4
  healthy eating, 150–2
  higher prices, projected, 200–1
  meat, 145–7
  meat consumption, reduction in, 148, 150
  oats and barley, 144–5
  pre-war Germany, shortage in, 74–5, 77
  productivity, 23
  rice, 136–7, 143–4
  rye, 140
  shortages, 23
  triticale, 141
  vegetables, 151
  war, in, 148–9
  wheat, 138–40
Forrester, Jay W., 17
France
  assignat, end of, 69–70
  deflation, 1930s, 65–6
  gold standard, abandonment of, 66
  inflation scenario, 68–70
franchising, 160–3, 183–5
Franklin, Benjamin, 28
Fyldes, Christopher, 119

GATT talks, breakdown of, 57
Germany
  financial crisis, response to, 55
  inflationary pressures, 81
  liquidation in, 74
  nationalism in, 46
  pre-war. See pre-war Germany
goats, 147
gold standard
  departure from, 38–9
  France, abandoned by, 66
  meaning, 85
  stabilizing effects of, 85–6
  US dollar leaving, 173
government
  agencies, accounting systems, 86
  bonds, yield on, 47
  borrowing, 84
  changing attitudes to, 201
  private-sector agencies, creation of, 85
  revenue base, fragmentation in,

201–2
waste, reduction in, 86
Grace Commission, 43, 86
grains, 136–7
Great Depression, 1–3
Greenhouse Effect, 24
Groundwork Trust (GT), 107, 110–12, 114, 117

Halifax Building Society, 120–1, 124
Handy, Charles, 160, 166–7
health
  costs, cutting, 87–8
  efficient running of, 90
  New Zealand, in, 87–9
  Oregon, financing in, 88–9
  transfer of cost, 87
Hitler, Adolf, 77
Home Owners Loan Corporation (HOLC), 122, 129
home workers, 163–5
Hoover, Herbert, 40, 60, 64
housing
  American rescue package, 131–2
  cycles, 122
  fall in prices, 120–1, 123
  home ownership, encouragement of, 122
  investment in, 119–20, 123
  Kondratieff trough, effect of, 122
  Kuznets cycle. See Kuznets cycle
  low-rent occupation, for, 130
  meltdown, avoiding, 129–31
  mortgages. See mortgages
  National Home Owners Relief Fund (NHORF), 133–4
  rented accommodation, decrease in, 122
  repossessed, 44, 62
  repossession process, 124–7
  stamp duty holiday, 129
  US, crash in, 14
Howell, Ralph, 101–3

Imperial Preference, 59
income tax
  administrative reform, 87
  income from, fall in, 95–6
  negative, 87

India
  grain drain, 136–7
inflation
  advance warning of, 176
  debt, 9, 44
  debts, reducing, 66–7
  effect of, 67
  ending of, 68
  initiation of, 191
  investment in, 191–2
  rising, higher interest rates to check, 9
  scenario, examples of, 68–9
  short-term interest rates, quelled by increasing, 67–8
insolvency
  pending, signs of, 155–6
interest rates
  corporate debt, effect on, 174–5
  inflation phase, in, 192
  rock bottom, at, 5
  short-term
    increase quelling inflation, 67–8
    raising, 57
  uneven movement of, 11
  US, effect of rise in, 2
investment
  crisis, through, 190–4
  depression phase, in, 194
  Eurodollar interest rate futures, in, 191
  fixed interest securities, in, 191
  inflation phase, in, 191–2
  liquidation, in, 192–4
  long-term bonds, in, 193
  recovery stocks, 196–8
  resource stocks, 194–6
  soft-trade commodities, in, 192
investors
  business-cycle recession, in, 189
  US economy, keeping eye on, 189

Japan
  consumer debt, 43
  economy, downturn in, 45
jet stream, 25
Jordan, Michael, 155
Juglar cycle, 8, 10
  crisis phase, 12

current, end of, 13
fresh, beginning of, 199
Great War, following, 13
identification of, 11
intensity of, 13
liquidation phase, 12–13
phases of, 11
prosperity phase, 11–12
recession phase, 13
record of, 47–8
Juglar, Clement, 11

Kondratieff cycle, 11, 122
Browning food cycle, relationship
with, 31
dry period, lows coinciding with, 22
fresh, beginning of, 199
identification of, 16
last low point in, 120
long wave, as, 16–17
lows, examination of, 35
next low point of, 15
peaks and troughs, 17–18
present, 18–19
upwave of, 17
Kondratieff, Nicolai, 16
Krakatau, eruption of, 27–9
Kuznets cycle, 11, 122
earliest low point, 14
identification of, 14
low point, crop failures, 41
lunar precession cycle, as, 15
momentum, 14
next low point of, 15
Kuznets, Simon, 14

Lakagigar, eruption of, 27–8, 35
Lamont, Norman, 10, 129
lifestyle, changes in, 200–1
liquidation
assets, of, 68
beginning of, 193
Germany, in, 74
inflation, after, 68
investment in, 192–4
Juglar cycle, phase of, 12–13
preparation for, 177
Little Ice Age, 33, 98
Local Government Act 1988

compulsory competitive tendering,
85, 169–71
long wave
history, in, 17–19
maximum length of, 19
world economy, in, 16–17
lunar precession cycle, 15

Mackie, Bill, 155
Ming dynasty, 33
mismanagement, 155–6
commercial misjudgment, 178
correcting, 178–81
monetizing debt, 66–7
mortgages
capital repayment, 123
clusters, corporations buying, 132
deferred interest, 126
endowment, 124
increase in number of, 120
National Home Owners Relief Fund
(NHORF), 133–4
negative equity, 124, 132
partial repayments, 128
repayment period, lengthening of
term, 126
repossession process, 124–7
securitizing, 132–3

national debt default, 57
National Home Owners Relief Fund
(NHORF), 133–4
National Recovery Administration
(NRA), 60, 62
National Vocational Qualifications
(NVQ), 116
natural cycles, 8
Nevado del Ruiz, eruption of, 29
New Zealand
health and education costs, 87–9
Notgeld, 77

office space, excess of, 8–9
oil and gas supplies, 47

Pacific Rim, volcanoes in, 30
pigs, 147
Pinatubo, eruption of, 24–6, 52, 135
politicians

climatic matters, ignorance of, 22
depressions, role in, 1–2
Poor Laws, 98
Poor Rate, 99
population
 increasing, effect on economy, 23
poultry, 147
pre-war Germany
 asset-backed currency, idea for, 77
 barter, prevalence of, 76
 currency, issue of, 76
 effects of collapse, 79–80
 food, shortage of, 74–5, 77
 foreign exchange speculators, 74
 government finances, stabilization of,
  77–8
 Great War, financing, 71
 inflation scenario, 70–80
 Rhineland, occupation of, 75–6
procurement procedures, 86
property
 fall in prices, 120–1, 123
 house price/earnings ratio, 120
 investment in, 119
prosperity
 Juglar cycle, phase of, 11–12
public expenditure
 cutbacks in, 82–4
 significant items of, 83
 United States, in, 83–4
public industries, privatization of, 85
public sector pay, decrease in, 87
Public Works Administration (PWA),
 62–3
Pugsley, J.
 'deadly anomaly', 50
 Interest Rate Strategy, 50

rainfall
 too little, effect of, 21
Rank Xerox, reconstruction of, 163–6
recession
 Juglar cycle, phase of, 12–13
 specialist work, options for, 185
Reconstruction Finance
 Corporation (RFC), 61, 64
recovery management, 157–9
refugees
 famine, from 4

Reichsbank
 September 1930, run on, 37–8
Rentenmark, 77–80
Resolution Trust Corporation (RTC),
 132
Richardson, Ruth, 88
Roggenmark, 74, 77
Roosevelt, Franklin D., 40, 60–1, 103,
 122, 129–31, 134
Rostow, W. W., 16
rural electricity programme, 86
Russia
 fascist political parties in, 46

San Andreas Fault, 30
Santayana, George, 2
Schacht, Dr Hjalmar, 77–9
Schumpeter, Joseph, 11, 16, 155
self-employment, increase in, 200, 202
SHAC, London housing-aid centre,
 125, 128
shamrock organizations
 FI Group, 168–9
 meaning, 160
 principle behind, 166
 public sector, in, 169–71
 structure, 166–8
 subcontractors, 167–8
sheep, 147
small businesses, 91
Small Firms Loan Guarantee Scheme
 (SFLGS), 92–3
Smoot–Hawley Tariff Act, 4, 40, 58, 64
Stalin, Joseph, 16
state, power of, 3
stock-markets, uneven movement of, 11
Stockman, David, 99
sunspots, 31–3
Sweden, unemployment insurance,
 100–1
Switzerland, unemployment insurance,
 100

T-bill yield, 49
T-bonds
 CRB Index, relationship with, 51
 rising yield on, 67
 yields, 48–50, 64
Tambora, eruption of, 26–7, 33

tariff protection, 4
technology
  employment patterns, effect on, 200
Thompson, Dr Louis, 15
travelling, decrease in, 201
triticale, 141

unemployed
  completion of work to specification,
    117
  conservation work by, 107–10
  organization of projects for, 111–13
  planning projects for, 113–16
  training opportunities for, 116
  urban projects, 107, 110–12
unemployment
  approaches to, 99–101
  Civilian Conservation Corps (CCC),
    concept of, 97–8, 103–7
  community programmes, 98
  education aptitude, evaluation of, 100
  insurance, 100–1
  level of, 95, 97
  planning for, 113
  state support, work in exchange for, 100
  training, 96
  work creation programmes, 97
  workfare, 100
unemployment benefit
  burden of, 101
  funding, 96
  work in return for, 101–3
United States
  bank 'holiday', 61
  budget deficit, 83–4
  debt to GNP ratio, 40
  devaluation, 61
  development projects, 63
  economy
    boosting, 39
    scenarios for, 190
  education aptitude, evaluation of, 100
  Emergency Farm Mortgage Act
    (EFMA), 62
  Federal Deposit Insurance
    Corporation (FDIC), 61
  Grace Commission, 43, 86
  grain drain, 136
  Home Owners Loan Corporation

  (HOLC), 62
  New Deal, 61–3, 65, 93, 98
  Oregon, health care in, 88–9
  presidents, election of, 40
  recovery, 1930s, 59–63
  repossessed housing, 44, 62
  savings and loan institutions, 43–4,
    131
  wheat, output of, 32
  workfare, 100
US dollar
  gold standard, leaving, 173
  world's reserve currency, as, 2, 48
US government
  debts, 42–3
  guarantees by, 9
  history, paying close regard to, 56

value added tax, reclaim of, 202
Versailles Treaty, 71
volcanic eruptions, effect of, 135
  Asama, 28
  Azul, 27
  Bezymianny, 52
  Cosiguina, 28
  CRB Index as indicator of, 52–3
  El Chicon, 52
  Fuego, 52
  Krakatau, 27–9
  Lakagigar, 27–8, 36
  Mount St Helens, 52
  Nevado del Riuz, 29, 52
  Pinatubo, 24–6, 52, 135
  Tambora, 26–7, 33
  Tarawera, 27
  Tiatia, 52

weather
  matters affecting, 22
  patterns, change in, 23–4
  volcanic eruptions, effect of, 24–9
Wheeler cycle, 11
Wheeler, Raymond, 11, 34–6, 202
White, Michael, 44
Woolton, Lord, 149
work and training packages
  unemployed, for, 4
working environment, changes in, 200

180-year sun-retrograde cycle, 11, 33–4

Warner now offers an exciting range of quality titles by both established and new authors. All of the books in this series are available from:
Little, Brown and Company (UK) Limited,
P.O. Box 11,
Falmouth,
Cornwall TR10 9EN.

Alternatively you may fax your order to the above address. Fax No. 0326 376423.

Payments can be made as follows: Cheque, postal order (payable to Little, Brown and Company) or by credit cards, Visa/Access. Do not send cash or currency. UK customers: and B.F.P.O.: please send a cheque or postal order (no currency) and allow £1.00 for postage and packing for the first book, plus 50p for the second book, plus 30p for each additional book up to a maximum charge of £3.00 (7 books plus).

Overseas customers including Ireland, please allow £2.00 for postage and packing for the first book, plus £1.00 for the second book, plus 50p for each additional book.

NAME (Block Letters) ....

ADDRESS...

....

☐ I enclose my remittance for _____

☐ I wish to pay by Access/Visa Card

Number ☐☐☐☐☐☐☐☐☐☐☐☐☐☐☐☐

Card Expiry Date ☐☐☐☐